Operation Stormfront

From Weatherman
To Wall Street

Author:
Dr. Terry Oroszi

Greylander Press

Operation Stormfront: From Weatherman to Wall Street

ISBN:978-0-9821683-6-3

This book is dedicated to my family.

Table of Contents

Chapter One

Coffee, Black, no Sugar

The benefit of drinking coffee black is that you get your order immediately, without giving your name, or waiting in the line with all the fancy-coffee-drinkers. By the time it was Eve's turn to order, her impatience was clear to everyone around her. Before the barista had a chance to ask her what she wanted, Eve interrupted, giving her order using as few words as possible. Eve's tension was concentrated in her face and neck, and a glance at the clock propelled it into her shoulders.

The barista, a black-haired, heavily pierced teenager,

in a charcoal tee and skinny jeans, handed Eve her drink without meeting her eyes. He displayed a nervousness in his hands that made her wonder how he managed to do so without spilling the drink all over the counter. His "Thank you ma'am" went unnoticed, thanks to Eve's ability to zone out people that she deemed uninteresting or unworthy of her attention. Her disconnect from society served her well in her line of work.

Eve maneuvered her way through the early-morning crowd of coffee worshippers; it wasn't hard. Her pinched expression and narrowing eyes caused people to get out of her way, and when that didn't fix the problem, a casual opening of the jacket to show off her Glock usually did. She knew that trick with the gun would not be sanctioned by the FBI, but when she was in a pre-coffee mood, she didn't care.

Eve preferred Starbucks's solid wood chairs to the comfy, overstuffed, leather sofas. The deep cushions and soft upholstery allowed a person to get a little too relaxed for her comfort. Exhibiting anything close to comfortable in public was something she scorned. This she had learned from her father, not from her experience as an FBI agent in counterintelligence.

Unfortunately, she was in such a hurry to get away from the crowd that she carelessly splashed hot coffee down her shirt. She was not overly concerned; a small amount of her paycheck actually went to improve her laughable wardrobe. Eve's clothing had one purpose, to assist her in blending into her surroundings. A cute twenty-something man handed Eve a napkin. She forced a smile on her face before taking the napkin, adding a nod of thanks, and turning before he had a chance to speak. Then she found her seat, off in a corner away from others, near the bathrooms and the back exit. Eve sat down, closed her eyes and took a deep breath before she took her first sip. She felt a tingling warmth in her limbs and the tension started to slip away.

The ambiance of coffee houses made them her home away from home. The usual hum of voices and click of laptop keyboards could be heard only slightly above the harsh grinding of the coffee machines and the annoying, often-too-peppy, voices of the baristas. She inhaled again; nothing could beat the aroma of bitter roasted coffee beans and the mellow jazz playing in the background. Eve was starting to feel like a human and the burgeoning smile on her face was one of pleasure and contentment.

She looked around at the chalk artwork and wondered if someone at the store was really this creative or if they were purchased with the art already drawn. Eve had never thought of herself as creative, at least not in terms of art, but boy did she know how to spin a story to get out of trouble.

Overly caffeinated customers would regularly pass by her table and try to strike up a conversation. Despite her constant attempts to blend in, Eve was an unpretentious natural beauty, and the coffee shop crowd appreciated her makeup-free face, her long auburn locks and alabaster skin. All it took was one penetrating, non-blinking stare from Eve to ward off even the most confident of men.

She developed her sense of awareness from her father, but her looks came from her mother. When Eve looked in the mirror, she saw her mother looking back. In fact, wearing her hair long aided in recreating that reflective memory and why she kept it so. Eve, born Evelyn Marie Black, last saw her mother when she was five years old. The memory of her mother was one likened to an angel. Her mother was beautiful, tall, and slender, whereas Eve was of average height, and a little curvy. Her curves stemmed from her utter aversion to cooking and dirty dishes. If she could eat out and the food was fast, then life was good, if the food was tasty, even better.

Her parents met on the Ann Arbor campus of the University of Michigan. Her mother, Alice, a Kappa Delta sorority girl, met John, her father, when he was protesting the current government on the plaza outside Hill Auditorium. He stood there speaking, gesturing for emphasis, surrounded by students talking and laughing, lawn mowers, and birds chirping, looking like a God.

John was unlike the men Alice normally dated. She kept her circle Greek, dating only guys from her brother fraternity, and when not dating KD brothers, Alice was deep in conversation about them with her sorority sisters. Add shopping and attending an occasional class, and that made up her college life.

John, on the other hand, looked like a scholarship boy in faded blue jeans and worn leather sandals. He stood on a flipped milk crate, sans shirt, showing off a well-defined, sun-tanned body. Despite his unrefined appearance, he spoke with confidence and passion about a different society, socialism, and the Weather Underground.

Alice had no interest in politics, but his visual appeal

proved magnetic. She found herself returning to the plaza day after day, hoping he would notice, and he did. On one particularly beautiful fall day, John stepped off his crate, crossed the sidewalks and onto the grassy lawn where she stood. He wrapped his arms around her and planted on her unsuspecting mouth, a lingering, toe-tingling, kiss, unlike anything she had ever experienced. Then he looked into her eyes and told her they would marry one day. Alice flushed, feeling lightheaded and unable to breath. When he released her, she felt faint and started to fall. He reached out his arms to steady her. John smelled of fresh lawns, wet earth, and coffee. The world around them melted away, it was just the two of them. A cool wind blew across her skin and she shivered, unsure if it was the wind, him, or both. He pulled her in tighter and they stayed in a near embrace for what felt like hours.

To call it a whirlwind romance would be accurate. They would meet for lunch on the quad and watched the chaos around them. She would lay her head on his lap and he would stroke her hair, speaking to her in hushed whispers about life, his plans, and how much he adored his beautiful Alice. Occasionally this idyllic scene was interrupted by hordes of students throwing Frisbees, footballs, and once, even a beer bottle.

John had a one-room apartment that served as a retreat for the new couple, with its gray weathered walls, broken window blinds and no curtains. There they found privacy not available in her sorority house. The sparse furniture looked like something you would find on the side of the road on garbage day, and a loud, whirring ceiling fan made you feel the need to raise your voice to be heard. Over the next few weeks, they rarely left the room. Time seemed to stand still, and Alice felt safe and whole when she was with him. The mismatched couple continued to keep to themselves, both knowing the criticism they would receive from friends.

When Alice found herself pregnant, her parents demanded a quick courthouse marriage and Alice's departure from college. They didn't approve of John, but a poorly matched marriage was better than an unmarried, pregnant daughter. Alice moved into John's place, painted the walls, added curtains to the windows, and managed to convince John that throw pillows for the sofa were a necessity. As Alice's belly grew, she started to resent her life. Her sorority sisters abandoned her, and with little money, it was hard to go shopping or have fun. She pleaded with her parents to help, but they maintained that Alice needed to pay for her bad decisions and ignored her pleas.

John was offered a graduate teaching assistant position in the engineering department. The salary he earned wasn't enough to support his new family, so he worked in his advisor's laboratory during the day and created recruiting pamphlets for the Weather Underground in the evening.

The young family moved into a rental home near campus. When the baby was born, Alice felt she had a purpose again. Although they didn't have much, they were happy. Her old sorority sisters held a baby shower for her and cooed over the cuteness of her baby girl. Alice knew that when John got his Ph.D. their life would improve, and she would be able to return to school. This went on for another two years.

In October of 1969, John left his wife and little girl to join his brothers and sisters in Chicago to protest the Vietnam War. John knew this political standoff would upset his sorority wife, but not as much as his arrest for his part in the Days of Rage demonstration.

When he returned home to Michigan, Alice and John's time together was strained. Their daughter was in preschool and Alice spent her days cleaning, cooking, and missing her friends. In just two years, the Weathermen went from a socialist campus group to a designated terror organization. John was one of the Weathermen Leaders who made it onto the FBI most wanted list.

One hot summer day, five-year-old Evie (a nickname chosen by her parents) was in her wading pool. She was teaching her doll how to swim. Alice lounged nearby soaking up the sun, her eyes closed and possibly asleep. Her daddy showed up and abruptly said they had to go away. Life was never the same. Evie had to leave her doll laying on the ground, hair matted and drying. The tiny clothes hanging on a jump-rope-turned-clothes-line, never to be seen again.

For the next several weeks they, under no circumstances, spent more than a couple days at one location before having to shuffle to another. Usually, it was to a stranger's home, so little Evie never had a bedroom and was constantly being told to quiet down. When they ran out of John's associates to stay with, they started staying at run down, low-cost motels. Evie didn't mind the motels because it was just the three of them, Mommy, Daddy, and Evie. She could jump on the beds, eat junk food, and watch cartoons. Evie was starting to believe in happiness again.

On a day that seemed like any other day, Alice said she couldn't take it anymore and left Evie and John in a motel outside Western Springs, Illinois. Evie never saw her mother again. She was only five, but she always carried the memory of that day as if it had just happened. The room was maroon, with flowered pillowcases, and lime green shag carpet.

The air conditioner cooled the room quickly and moments before her life changed, Evie had wrapped a towel around her neck, like a cape, and jumped on the bed exclaiming loudly that she was superwoman. Her mother was holding a bulging bag and leaned in to kiss her little girl gently, with tears in her eyes. She started to leave and then turned in the doorway to get a last look at her Evie. The sun shone through the open door behind her mother. Evie thought she looked like an angel. She bounced on the bed, cape floating around her shoulders, "Bye Mommy!" Evie had no way of knowing the significance of the moment. Then the door shut, and her daddy sat on the edge of the bed and cried.

The crying went on for several days, but it felt like forever to a five-year-old. Then one day her daddy's friend showed up in an old pickup and took them away from the motel and the cartoons, and the sadness. She suspected they were heading to where her mommy was hiding, but she was wrong. She pleaded with her daddy to take her to mommy, over and over. Tears were shed every morning and every night, by them both.

Daddy came and went on important business. Evie

was left to her own devises and spent her days imagining what it would be like when they found Mommy. She tried to make friends with the mice that raided their meager pantry until the day her daddy brought back a little puppy. Evie had a new best friend. She named him Sebastian, because she felt a little puppy needed a big name. He put a smile on her face and made her laugh again, at least for a few months.

She was once more wrenched away. They were on the move again, and this time it was Sebastian who was left behind. They spent many days in an old rusty RV that John had managed to buy with what little money he had. On their journey, John spoke to Eve about the desert they would encounter, about the mountains, and forests, the hikes they could go on, and the friends she would soon make. Eve looked out the window and remained silent.

John and Evie ended up north of Taos, New Mexico. When they reached what was to be their new home, she saw familiar places like her beloved fast-food restaurants and Wal-Mart. Their final stop was at the Taos Inn. The excitement of the journey was over, and she missed her puppy terribly. Evie's father had several Weatherman friends at the Inn, and the next morning, the group caravanned into the desert. John and Evie had the RV, some had campers, and others, just tents. They made this new state their home and Eve lived there until she moved to New York for college.

Life in the desert wasn't easy, but fortunately, the location was close enough to the real world that getting electricity and other comforts took the small troupe less than a year. The group called themselves

"Socialism For Humanity," SFH for short. Years later the make-shift community grew roots and became a small village known as Tres Piedras. SFH members, mostly college graduates dissatisfied with their previous life and their peer's money-fueled ambitions, believed by creating this new home that they were freeing people from domination and greed. Their New Mexico desert homeland would allow individuals to flourish mentally and fill the holes in their souls with creativity and loving connections.

Eve was ten when her future stepmother, Camilla, arrived at the camp for a visit with a college chum. Camilla was not beautiful in the same way as Eve's Scandinavian mother, she had unruly dark hair that looked rarely combed. She was well-rounded and wore exotic clothes from her native Mexico. She always had a big smile and her huge, sparkling, brown eyes nearly disappeared when she laughed. When Camilla wrapped her arms around Eve, she felt love like no other; she felt like she was home.

John had chosen this New Mexico desert location because of a Cold War bunker located on the property. It was a place he could escape to quickly if the police or feds showed up looking for him. The bunker could be used as an underground storm shelter, supporting a large family for several days. It had a reinforced hatch entrance with a corrugated metal cap that hid the stairs descending into the bunker. The white and overly bright fluorescent lights constantly flickered and if in there too long a person could feel quite claustrophobic. The remnants of the cold war were all around the space, including a small toilet complete with a hand pump, and sleeping bunks. Across one wall stood a row of storage cabinets with ammunition, medical supplies, food, and easy access to racks of weapons. John had carved himself a small living area, complete with a sleeping bag, radio, microwave, and fridge. This came in handy on those nights when he drank so much, he could not make it up the stairs. The outer wall had floor to ceiling shelves with cans of food, many with the labels removed. Next to the cans were boxes of military MREs (meals ready to eat).

At the end of the bunker was a large mural of the historic Hispanic village of Tularosa. The landscape of the village gave the viewer a close look at the atomic bomb exploding in the desolate New Mexico desert. License plates from the 1950s and 1960s were hung on the walls and added a little color to the drab space. The isolated feel of the space was accentuated by the artificial hum of an oscillating fan. After a few years of using it as food storage, John had become interested in a new technology, the microcomputer, and had parts scattered throughout the confined space. He spent all his days inside the bunker with a bottle, building computers and drinking. After a drink or two, the canned air smell would fade and what remained was the faint odor of sweat, stale food, and gunpowder. On those rare moments when Evie was allowed inside, she would make tents out of the bunk beds and fall asleep.

Before Camilla, Evie's father would often forget to eat or sleep and left the care of his daughter up to the other members of the community. Camilla's presence and patience worked their magic on him as it had on

Evie. She created structure in their life, something to which both John and Evie were unaccustomed.

After one of her many mini vacations to see her family in Mexico, Camilla returned home with a rescue puppy, hoping to relieve the sadness Evie carried from leaving her puppy behind so many years ago. Evie fell in love instantly. She called this new dog Sebastian as well, Seba for short. Seba was a Xolo, a Mexican Hairless dog. He was copper and white, with large bat-like ears, too big for his face. A long elegant neck and a Mohawk-like tuft of fur atop his head added to his uniqueness. He quickly became Evie's new best friend.

Camilla was a terrific cook and at any time of the day, her kitchen was full of tortillas, spicy chilies, and she would be either humming to herself or chatting with hungry neighbors popping by for a visit and a chance at home cooking. Their voices were raised due to the refrigerator motor rumbling and pot lids banging. There was clutter everywhere, but it was organized clutter, that added to the homey feeling rather than turning people away from the cozy hearth of the mobile home.

The kitchen was Seba's second favorite spot, the bunker being his first. He had a plaid blanket next to his food bowl and was always on the lookout for falling scraps when Camilla prepared food. They would often not even have a chance to hit the linoleum floor of the old RV before he had it in his mouth and was quietly begging for more. Between Seba and Camilla's due diligence, one would never find a crumb or cobweb in their home.

17

Camilla allowed John to spend no more than half the day hiding away in his bunker. She treated it like a job, not as an escape. Soon the alcoholic retreat became a place for John to work clear-headed, and his drinking was reserved for social time in the company of his family and good neighbors.

It was at the kitchen table where Evie spent her days studying and snacking on homemade cookies. She would look for any excuse to escape into the desert with only a book as a companion. Outside the compound, the sand and rock landscape were dotted with cacti. By the age of ten, Eve could name them all: the tall saguaros, the barrel, and the prickly pear. She would find a shaded rock under an acacia tree and disappear into books about faraway places, like Philadelphia, Florida, and San Francisco.

Inside her little room she had a treasure box full of weathered glass, bleached bones, and other desert finds. She would occasionally arrive home with a pet snake, lizard, or injured baby jackrabbit and they would occupy her for a short while before Camilla released them.

A water bottle was always at her side as the grit and dust would dry out her mouth very quickly. She would drink it sparingly for she knew that when the water was gone, she would have to return home to the kitchen table and her schoolwork. Occasionally, Evie would see visitors off in the distance. When this happened she would drop everything and run home as fast as she could. Her fight or flight instinct would kick in, excitement and fear overwhelming her senses and sweat dripping into her eyes by the time she made it back to the village. She would sound the alarm to the SFH crows that there were "strangers" nearby. The warning would send the entire village into a state of anxiety and vigilance until the strangers left their lands.

Periodically, the police would show up. John would hide out in the bunker until they left. It was unknown to the rest of the group whether they were looking for John specifically, but no one questioned his insistence on hiding in the bunker, and no one revealed his presence.

Visitors to the area were typically harmless and ranged from people who loved the outdoors, survivalists or teens looking to let off some steam, to the infrequent tourist, afraid they would become food for the desert predators. Real trouble came when the dry riverbeds flooded in the rainy season. The desert wildlife would have their routines interrupted and this caused them to be more dangerous than at any other time of the year.

Evie spent as much time as possible outdoors, but the rainy season affected the SFH group as much as it did the wild animals. They were evolving from a transient lifestyle, living in RVs and tents, to one more grounded, taking advantage of the woods nearby and working with their hands to create something stable and long-lasting.

When Evie was thirteen, John created for her an outdoor cabana-like bedroom, that was secure from predators, and attached to the RV, but gave her the feel of her own space. The ceiling was really an umbrella-like roof that could be opened to the night sky and closed against the hot desert sun. For her birthday, the community had pooled their resources and purchased for her a Swift Model 831 Telescope, and she would spend her nights looking up at the sky.

The floor of her room was covered with rugs, many of them she made herself, the others were gifts from her neighbors. She had a small twin bed, a dresser with drawers that were so difficult to open she found herself keeping her clothes on top rather than inside.

Something obviously lacking in this teen bedroom were walls plastered with posters of movie stars. Without the influence of television, the children and teens of the community were not enamored of Hollywood's idea of perfection. What the adults of the SFH had not considered when they collectively decided to ban T.V. was the impact it would have on their children's understanding of cultural references and connection to the outside world.

Evie's pride and joy was her record player and collection of albums. Her music choices stemmed from the favorites of the adults in the community, the Rolling Stones, Marvin Gaye, Muddy Waters, and Iggy Pop. But it was Nina Simon, American singer, songwriter, and civil rights activist, that became her go-to choice. The poetry in her music fit Evie's varied emotions. Evie had few friends and had to come up with ways to entertain herself.

While the idea of a bedroom like this sounds appealing, the sand manages to make its way in through every possible crevasse, and Evie dreamt that one day, she would wake buried in sand never to be found again. On those nights, she would grab her pillow and blanket and make her way inside and onto the sofa. After a fitful sleep, she would wake later than usual to the smell of chorizo sizzling in the pan, baked eggs, and fresh squeezed orange juice.

The community of like-minded friends interacted more like an extended family than neighbors, due to the closeness of their homes and the sharing of limited resources. They still experienced arguments and fights, but they would mend the rifts after a time and once again come together. In the center of their land was a communal space where they would gather in the evenings. It was not unusual to have a community member break into song and have others chime in, singing along.

One of the first structures they built was a schoolhouse for the younger children that could serve as a meeting space when the weather was bad, and a sleeping space for welcomed visitors. Evie earned a little money working with the children, giving the teachers a much-deserved break. She read Jane Austin, Charles Dickens, and all the classics, before switching to addition/subtraction and algebra. Her favorite part of being the teacher's aid was the creative time, when they would draw, paint, or go on hikes to learn about the flora and fauna found in the desert and nearby forests.

When Evie was fourteen, her father brought her down into the bunker and started teaching her about computers. This soon became her favorite lesson of the day. Evie was fascinated and shared with him that she wanted to learn everything she could about computers, but what she really craved was the closeness with her father. His approval meant the world to her. He introduced her to the internet, which took her to exotic places and introduced her to many different types of people. When she surfed the web, she was able to get away from her isolated community and become acquainted with the rest of the world.

The SFH kept a close watch on the people in the surrounding areas. Their fear and distrust of the government caused them to be wary of any outsider. When it was Evie's turn to go to the nearby town for supplies, she thought of it as an adventure. The grocery store, with its bright bulbs, gave the illusion of daytime, all the time. The exposed metal shelving and well-worn linoleum aisles stocked with food products, many that she had never seen nor tasted, gave her a lifetime interest in food. The smell of warm bread from the bakery reminded Evie of home and was instantly calming. Her favorite space within the store was the produce area. She would sneak a few grapes whenever she passed them, marveling at the coolness of the fruit, and enjoying the splash of sweetness when the skin burst in her mouth.

The euphoria of the store would often be short-lived. Crying babies, toddlers throwing tantrums, women standing in front of open freezers creating microclimates and blocking the path, and the clanking of shopping carts were constant reminders that there were strangers about, and she had to be on guard. Evie learned early on to read people. She knew by interpreting their verbal and nonverbal cues how to react and stay safe.

An aggressive stance, clenching of fists and flaring nostrils were obvious signs of anger, but it was the more subtle signs, like the tightness in the eyes, a raised chin when speaking, flexing of the fingers that were often overlooked by most people. Evie knew she displayed her own nonverbal gestures that would alert others as to how she was feeling. Biting her lip, running fingers through her hair, and fidgeting were the tells that Evie displayed, indicating that she didn't fit in when she was outside of SFH.

Being surrounded by outsiders initially scared her. She was intimidated by the ease with which they walked down streets, their unconcerned patience as they stood in crowded checkout lines; and she was bewildered by their constant smiling. Eventually, Evie became quite good at mimicking the townies and believed that, in their eyes, she looked like she belonged. Inside, she knew she was different. Living in a small community didn't help her social skills, but her intellect was quite advanced. One advantage of growing up without television was that Evie always had a book in her hand, and several more waiting.

When Evie was seventeen years old, Camilla entered her room with a handful of college applications and SAT studying materials. Without conferring with John, she scheduled Evie to take the SAT in Taos. Evie was conflicted. She was afraid to leave home, having never attended a real school. Evie believed she was inadequate and less prepared than others her age. She also knew the power of an advanced education, with nearly 100% of the SFH group having advanced degrees, going away to college was understood as a necessity.

One of the pamphlets was of particular interest to Eve. It was Columbia University's Department of Psychology. Eve didn't want to heal people, or even to help people. She wanted to learn how to control them; how to get them to do what she wanted. Eve recognized her insatiable need to control everything and everyone she came into contact with. There was no chance she was going to let anyone hurt her. She wanted to avoid the pain of losing people, like her mother or even her ever-so-distant father. She was determined to take control of each and everything in her life.

John wanted Eve to go to the University of New Mexico and insisted their Psychology program would be just as good, but when Eve was awarded a full scholarship to Columbia, he conceded and supported her decision. The cost was not his only concern. He didn't want his only daughter to be across the country. Albuquerque was only a two-hour drive. To Eve, the distance was part of the appeal. She knew she needed to be out in the real world if she were to achieve her goals.

A loud crash from behind the coffee counter brought Eve back to the present and she was reminded of her plans for the day. She needed to head to the office to meet Vic Stallion. Vic was an international arms dealer the FBI had managed to flip. His choices had been a long jail term or help the FBI get in with the arms and terrorism community. With a name like Vic, she had an idea of what she was in for: a dark-haired, overly muscled, but not-so-educated Italian. She laughed to herself. "He probably thinks he can win me over with his good looks and machismo." Little did he know that Eve had yet to meet a man, besides her father, who could intimidate her. That was not 100% true, her boss had a way of making her feel like a child.

Eve found that in both cases the respect she felt for the men was equal to their intimidation levels.

Eve gulped down the last of her coffee, cringing slightly at the taste of the now cool, dark, caffeinated liquid, and wished she had ordered a smaller size. As she made her way to the door, she did one last visual sweep of the room. No one seemed out of place. If they were looking at her, it had more to do with her obvious attitude and confidence, and not that they were out to get her.

Chapter Two

Armed and Dangerous

When Vic Stallion walked into the FBI interview room, he thought it resembled every stereotypical police station on TV, with cream-colored walls, paint peeling in the corners, evidence of past water leaks on the dropped ceiling, a reflective glass window on the wall and an old calendar the only decoration. The rickety table in the center of the room was full of papers and folders, and three chairs flanked the table, giving the space an air of asymmetry that offended his sense of balance. The room was so barren that Vic felt the echo of his breathing rather than hearing it. The air reeked of old coffee, cleaning products, and cigarette smoke. Despite the starkness, Vic could not shake the feeling that the room was unclean, and he immediately wished he was anywhere else. That was until he locked eyes with Eve. He was immediately struck by her beauty and confident demeanor. He stood a little taller, and sucked in his gut and thought to himself, "It's time to play a little game, see what she's got." When he sat down, he gave her the standard New Jersey "how you doin'" greeting. She just sat there and looked at him. This seedy little man may have an Italian name and hail from Jersey, but what immediately struck her as funny was that "Vic" was Indian, as in, from India. Vic was short in stature, round in waist and sported a thick head of dark hair. At least she had figured that right.

The silence continued for several minutes and he started getting worried, "Did this lady fall asleep with her eyes open? What the hell is wrong with her?" Vic thought to himself as he squirmed a bit in his seat. He was used to the shock people expressed when they first met him, the name, Vic Stallion conjured images of male porn stars, western cowboys, or east coast mafia, and he often used this to his advantage. He raised his voice and said, "Hey agent lady, are we going to have a conversation?" She just smiled, and that smile (you know the kind, doesn't reach the eyes) scared him. Vic, a man that spent his days with terrorists, selling them everything from hand grenades to missiles, felt like a naughty three-year-old boy under this woman's gaze.

He was not afraid to admit (to himself) that he was a little bit intimidated, was unsure of what would happen next, and wanted the hell out of there. He shifted a bit more in his seat and started to get up. The door opened and in walked a male in a suit and tie. Vic relaxed back down into his seat, "Ah, she was waiting for this guy." His attention immediately focused on the new player in this little game; and, oh, what a pompous man he was. His appearance was everything that screamed FBI: slick, athletic, handsome, tall and self-possessed. Vic entered him into his mental file under the moniker, Special Agent Dick.

The man sat down, pulled out paper and pen, and just as Vic expected him to speak, she did. "Mr. Stallion," she said, her deep raspy voice startling him, "I am Special Agent Eve Black, and this is my partner, Special Agent Beck, Sean Beck. Beck looked over at Vic and grunted a hello; he didn't look happy to be there and carried a bored look that appeared to shout that Vic was a waste of his time.

Vic did not respond to the agent's unintelligible grunt and just continued to look at the female and to what she was saying, "I need you to help me out, and in exchange, I will make your problems go away." Eve purposely used the pronoun "I" and not we. FBI agents are taught to use "We" to show the backing of the entire FBI organization when an agent spoke, but Eve wanted Mr. Stallion to be her informant, hers alone, not the FBI's. She ignored the stares from her former partner. He was a good agent, one of the best she had worked with, and would likely become the director of the FBI someday. Beck did not operate in a gray area, which was Eve's norm. He saw the world as black or white, guilty or innocent.

Over the past year, they had worked together to take

down a terror cell in the Midwest. The leader, Colton Smith, had managed to convince a group of young adults to blow up a bridge that connected two affluent communities. They wanted to highlight the inequality between the rich and poor by killing a few well-to-do individuals and disrupting their lives.

Fortunately, SA Beck was able to infiltrate the group, and was a voice of reason that Smith's followers heeded, and the cell disbanded. Smith, however, was not so easy to sway. He attempted to plant a bomb on his own. This decision did not come as a surprise to Beck or Black. Through an informant, they supplied Smith with an inert bomb. At the moment he planted the bomb, the FBI arrested him. The other members of the cell were never charged, and Eve was convinced that Beck had saved their lives. Their partnership was dissolved after the Smith case. She was going it alone on this one, but Eve wanted Beck to be in the interview room merely to demonstrate her power to the arms dealer.

Vic wanted to appear comfortable and in charge, but the sweat in his pits was out of control, and he needed a towel to wipe his face. He turned and looked at her. His response was embarrassingly timid. "Yes, ma'am?" Eve smiled to herself, but quickly caught it and turned it into a smirk. He was hers. She knew what to do. Break him down, then play on his weaknesses. "Vic, I need you to get me an invite to the International Defense Exhibition Conference (IDEC) being held this year in Cincinnati, Ohio. I want interviews arranged with the attendees on this list." She handed Vic a list of American terrorists who were not currently serving time, or dead.

"Well, ma'am, that will be a bit difficult, the IDEC

don't like feds, even when they look as good as you."

Eve's body went rigid and she wanted to punch this guy in the face. She thought to herself, "Always the looks. Men are fucking idiots, can't get beyond the breasts." Her disgust did not register on her face, but she knew she could use this. Men who were focused on her appearance always underestimated her.

She looked into his eyes and said, "Wrong answer Vic, you'll get me introductions, and this is how it's going to work."

Eve's plan was simple, Vic would arrange the meetings, encourage the terrorists to spend under thirty minutes with her, and in exchange they would each get ten thousand US dollars.

"Your plan is not a bad one, except, my apologies ma'am, one look at you and they will know you're not who you claim to be."

She glanced over at the man sitting next to her. He spoke for the first time, "We've got that covered."

Vic glanced down at the list, Mitch Weaver and his Unorganized Militia of Champaign County. He may be able to get him, but more likely he could convince Joshua Carter from the Michigan Hutaree Militia." Oh, to be a fly on the wall for that meeting!" he thought, chuckling inwardly. He would love to watch Special Agent Eve Black put Carter in his place.

The next group on the list was the Earth Liberation Front. He knew a guy who knew a guy, and he could make that work.

Vic continued down the list making mental notes and on occasion suggested replacements that he knew he could persuade. In short order, a plan was in place. Special Agent Black would show up at the conference under the guise of Dr. Nicole Mathers, a well-known academic, terrorist expert, researcher, and author. It would be up to the FBI to transform Eve's personality and style. Vic sensed that her soul was dark, her patience was low, and there was something innately wicked about her. He could not imagine her, making small talk with and gaining the confidence of the sort of people she would be meeting at the conference.

Vic was tired of the life he lived. He had children and a wife, and the stress he felt trying to keep them distanced from his day job was overwhelming. At the last weapons exchange he had arranged, Vyacheslav Ravonkov, a high-level mob boss from Russia, threatened to go after his family when Vic refused to sell him an EMP device that could devastate the US. Vic had the man poisoned, so he was no longer a threat, but there would always be men like Ravonkov. His family would always be in danger. Vic imagined what his life would be like if he could leave arms dealing behind for good. He had made plenty of money. Maybe now, this opportunity, was the time to step back, enjoy life, and watch Eve take down the others.

Chapter Three

Going Home

There are six ways to get from Brooklyn to Lower Manhattan: subway, bus, taxi, car, bike, or ferry. When traffic is good, the commute takes fifteen minutes, which is about the amount of time she needed to drink her coffee. Time is not really a big factor in Eve's choice of travel. Her priorities were comfort and peace of mind, which equated to the travel with the least amount of social interaction and communication.

On this particular morning, Eve received a call from Camilla, but the subway was too crowded to add to the noise with a phone conversation. A young man with body odor so bad she had to resist gagging, was playing a video game on his phone without using earphones. If she had to listen to the gurgling, pinging sounds of the game much longer, she was going to take that phone, and him, and throw them across the subway car. Nearby, a baby was crying, its stroller blocking the aisle. The oblivious mother was ignoring the wailing because she too was focused on her phone. Eve looked around at the filled bench seats, the passengers hanging on to the leather straps hanging from the ceiling with one hand, and a phone in the other.

Nearly everyone on the subway was hooked in, linked up, or Facebooking. She could be standing there in the nude and she was convinced not one person would notice. Maybe that was a slight exaggeration, but bloody hell, she hated people.

The constant opening and shutting of doors at every stop, the speakers crackling every time a destination was announced, and the press of people could be over-whelming. Eve had tried many methods over the years to cope with the external stimulus that would put her in a sensory overload. As a child she had the desert, but here in the city she had taken more drastic measures, first by taking drugs, then by learning how to meditate. If, in her daily commutes, there was physical contact with the fellow passengers, shoulders rubbing, hands groping, or any such touching, Eve would lose it.

When this happened, it took everything she had to not react with violence, and typically resulted in her making eye contact with the person, staring at them with a look on her face that caused them to shrink away in fear. At times like that, she missed her desert home more than ever. The landscape of sand, sunlight, and stone satisfied her need to be alone. The occasional screech of eagles far above served to increase the sense of space and isolation that soothed her. A bleak place that could suck the life out of most people reenergized Eve.

The copious amount of external stimulation was not something she was prepared for when she went off to college. Tres Piedras' population was smaller than some of her classes at Columbia. She had never experienced so much noise while living in the desert in New Mexico, and due to her estrangement from her father, her home was no longer a haven away from people and their inevitable noise.

Eve's father John had never forgiven her for joining the FBI and being part of the "Establishment." Not only was she part of the government, she had joined the very people that had been hunting her father and forced the family into a life on the run that caused her mother to leave them. The irony was not lost on Eve. The power that goes along with being part of the Federal Bureau of Investigation was occasionally worth the lack of father figure in her life, but she longed for his approval.

Leaving the desert for college in New York was Eve's choice. The scholarship she received paid for her room and board in addition to her classes, but she still had to take a part-time job to make it on her own. Because of Eve's disdain for human contact, she had no desire to join a sorority like her mother. Girls like that were confusing to Eve, but then again, almost everyone she met in college left her perplexed. Eve jockeyed between intrigued and alienated in most social situations.

The silly banter, the giggling, the intentional air of stupidity to appeal to men made no sense to her. It was almost as if these women were another species. Eve was determined to overcome her natural aversion to these behaviors and learn how to fit in, much like she had back home on the grocery runs. A good start, Eve had decided, was to engage in relationships with her college classmates. She managed to land a position as a bartender at 1020, the watering hole for the Columbia crowd. Here she could watch, learn and practice.

It was near lunchtime when Eve finally got around to calling Camilla back. She was shocked to hear her father, and not her stepmother, answer the phone. There was a long pause before she got around to responding, "Hello, Dad. It's been a long time. Camilla called..." Her father interrupted, "Evie, get out here, your mom is not well." He then immediately hung up the phone. Eve just sat there for a moment, processing. She grabbed her bag, and stopped only to let her boss, Special Agent in Charge (SAC) Adam Lange, know she needed to take a few days off.

SAC Lange ignored the urgency in her voice and said, "Evelyn, please," pointing to a chair across from his, "Sit down." Eve took a seat but was bouncing her leg and generally appeared quite anxious.

"So why do you have to fly to New Mexico?" He asked.

"Do you know a better way to travel that will get me there faster, sir?'

SAC Lange remembered now how frustrating it can be to talk with this woman. Exasperated he said, "I was referring not to the mode of travel, but to the reason for the trip and the time off."

"Well, sir, going out to New Mexico and returning often takes a couple days, and as far as the reason, it is regarding my stepmother."

SAC Lange inhaled, closed his eyes, counted to five, then exhaled, and thought perhaps if I just spell it out, I will get a straight answer, "Evelyn, what's wrong with your stepmother?"

"I don't know, sir, that's why I need the time off." I swear the man almost growled.

"Eve, is your stepmother sick?"

Eve looked at him with increased interest and leaned in, "Do you know something I don't know, sir?"

"Eve, get out of my office, now."

A very confused Eve left his office, left the building, and immediately hailed a taxi to take her to the airport. The ride was uneventful, and she was happy the driver did not attempt to have a conversation. Her primary dislike of taxis was the driver's belief that getting to know the passenger for the short time they were together would mean a bigger tip. In Eve's calculations, the tip decreased every time a driver uttered a word. She focused on her surroundings in an attempt to block out any emotions that might bubble to the surface. The driver had the radio tuned to pop music. The seats were well cared for, no stains nor trash on the floors. She noticed a coffee cup in the beverage holder and knew what her first stop would be once she arrived at the airport.

She walked through the automated glass doors

at La Guardia. In front of her were airline check-in counters, passengers queued up to get their tickets, she struggled to get to her airlines and ignored the lines, choosing instead to use the self-serve kiosk. Eve found it difficult not to bump into people, or to be bumped into, and her stress immediately increased to a dangerous level.

Over at the counter a well-dressed man was complaining about the lack of first-class seats, and how flying coach was not acceptable. It was difficult to not smile at the dissatisfaction of the patron. He struck her as an overbearing ass and imagined him in a middle seat, preferably between two chatty individuals.

With no bags to check, Eve's boarding process would be smooth and quick, but she was aware of the need for a few essentials. Eve strode into a Brookstone and bought a cheap carry-on; went next door to Afaze to buy a change of clothes, then into Hudson for toiletries. Unfortunately, with no Starbucks in sight, she had to settle for the Whole Bean coffee bar. The coffee wasn't bad, in fact, she might even have said it competed with Starbucks. She found passably comfortable, nearly quiet seating and waited for her gate to be called.

The flight was an uncomfortable one. She had a middle seat and was flying coach. Regardless of the size of the passengers flanking her, or even their attempts to mind their own business, Eve could never quite relax. In fact, flying coach was on her list of top five things to avoid. At one point, the man on her left leaned over just enough to feel her sidepiece and looked at her as if she were a possible terrorist. Eve just reached in her pocket, pulled out her badge, showed it to the concerned man, then slipped it back into her pocket without saying a word.

Eve would like to think her irritability was due to the stress she was feeling, but she was self-aware enough to know that "irritated" was her default state. The thought of seeing her father after so many years gave her a heavy feeling in the pit of her stomach. She had no idea what kind of reunion to expect. Her mind raced through possible scenarios. Worry for Camilla's health added to her unease, and with the next pass of the flight attendant, Eve ordered a Bloody Mary.

She once read that people ordered Bloody Mary's when flying because the sense of taste is blunted in flight. Sensations of sweet, salty, sour, and bitter all became dulled, however, the fifth flavor, savory umami, seemed to be unaffected by those in-flight inhibitors. Even amid loud noise and low pressure, the tongue can still taste the savory flavors of a Bloody Mary. She raised a mental toast to her taste buds and sipped her drink with her eyes closed. Seven hours after leaving New York, she was in New Mexico.

She had been lucky to get a seat near the front of the plane, so the wait to depart was minimal. That did not stop her from pushing past those in front of her, also waiting to get off the plane. She did not bother to create a plausible excuse because frankly, she did not care. The seven-hour confinement and the cacophony of post-flight phone conversations by her fellow passengers were too much for Eve. She had to disembark ASAP or there would be hell to pay.

It was a short walk to the Rent-A-Car where she got herself a hydro blue metallic Jeep Wrangler. The color was not important to her, it was the ability to take the top down and to spend the next thirty minutes utterly alone and in familiar territory that made this drive the best part of a miserable day. The smell of limestone, dusk and dried air was heaven. She vowed to seek out a candle with similar scents for her Brooklyn apartment.

The drive to Tres Piedras was peaceful. As she drove down highway sixty-four, she felt the years melt away. She knew each curve and bend in the road, some of them quite dangerous to those less familiar. Though the winding road had not changed, the landscape had altered quite a bit over the years. When she passed the Earthship visitor center, she laughed, remembering the late-night conversation with Camilla about her tête-à-tête with the Earthship's architect, Michael Reynolds. He was a visionary and painted a future that included a community of earth-berm homes made of tires collected from the desert highways. She and Camilla had always remained close despite her father's assertion that she was no longer his child.

Throughout Eve's traitorous career as an FBI agent, Camilla had maintained covert contact. Whenever Eve's father had gone off to his bunker to do his dark web whatever-the-hell-he-did, Camilla would call. The two women would be on the phone for hours, laughing and sharing tales. Camilla wanted stories about love interests, which Eve did not have. Instead, Eve would talk about recent cases and the total lack of intelligence most criminals displayed, ultimately leading to their arrest. Eve could not imagine her life without Camilla. She was the one tether to human emotion that Eve could indulge. The idea of the emptiness of a future without Camilla left her digging for tissues and created a heaviness in her chest that she could not control.

Her heart was near breaking and her vision blurred from crying when she reached Tres Piedras. She noted the new community center, which was once a school. The school had only eleven students when it closed in 2005. Camilla had worked so hard to make this center happen. Despite the high education level of the 300+ residents of Tres Piedras, very few of them lived above the poverty level, and to this day, few had running water or electricity. For most of the residents the community center was the only exposure and access to the internet. The village inhabitants, much like in their SFH days, did not consider money a priority. It came as no surprise that the community all pitched in to make the community center a reality because construction was the main occupation in Tres Piedras. The final structure was beautiful, a wooden one-story building with a park for children and pets. Seeing the children playing outside made the tears flow even more. Eve knew this was going to be a painful visit.

When she turned onto 285 and saw the Tres Piedras Railroad Water Tower, Eve knew she was home. It was just a minute or two before she was turning into the gravel driveway of her parent's property. The plants on the steps and faded boho flowers on the shutters reminded her of the day she and Camilla had painted their impressionist garden. They were wearing matching Old Navy overalls and Camilla let Evie choose the color of the flowers. It started out as one of her favorite days, until she took advantage of Camilla's quick trip inside for water. Evie decided she was big enough to climb the ladder, from which she subsequently fell. Camilla rarely scolded her, and this was no exception. She scooped Evie up, and soothed her with kisses and gentle talk as she carried her inside to wash and clean her scratches. Then she applied a generous number of Wonder Woman Band-Aids and pronounced her cured. Camilla then sat next to her on the sofa and pacified Evie with cookies and lemonade. They spent the rest of the afternoon reading Anne of Green Gables.

Eve had to compose herself before she got out of the car. She could not let her dad see her so emotional. She walked across the yard, thinking to herself that it needed a good mowing and surprised at the greenness of the space. The hiss of a nearby sprinkler warned her in time to dodge the droplets and she made it to the front of the house without an unplanned shower. Eve climbed the three steps and knocked on the peeling door of what was once her home. When no one answered she opened the door, walked inside, and yelled out, "Dad? I'm here!"

The first one to greet her was Seba. Shortly thereafter, her father emerged from the bedroom with a small suitcase, set it down by the door, and motioned for her to join him in the kitchen. Eve barely recognized her dad. His lanky physique, thick Sam Elliot moustache, deep, resonant voice, and western drawl, which fit so well with the New Mexico landscape, had been transformed into a haggard old man with lines around his eyes and a hungover, hopeless look.

He poured them both a cup of coffee. His shoulders

drooped, his spine bowed, and in a defeated monotone, he gave Eve the terrible news. "Evie, Camilla has been suffering from diabetes for the last few years and unbeknownst to me she started taking less than prescribed insulin due to costs and no healthcare. She lapsed into a coma yesterday and she was care-flighted to San Luis Valley Health Hospital in Alamosa, Colorado." As he said this, his shoulders started quaking and his eyes shone with waiting tears. Eve stood up, grabbed her chair and set it next to his. They both sat there in silence.

"Daddy...", that was all she could say. She wanted to say more; she wanted to put him at ease but found herself unable to do so.

He put her hand over hers and said, "As soon as you're ready, I want to take your mom a suitcase and a few of her favorite books so she will be ready when she wakes." Eve nodded with agreement. He stood and reached out to his baby girl, "I'm so sorry Evie."

She hugged him back, "Me too, daddy, me too." In an attempt to be strong John straightened up, took a step back and said, "Let's go."

Eve gulped down the last of her coffee and put her mug into the sink. There was no way she could handle one to two hours on the road without more. She opened the cabinet, grabbed a to-go cup, and filled it to the brim, before shutting off the coffee pot. Her father put the books into the suitcase, and together they closed up the house and hurried to the jeep.

The hospital was an hour and a half away and they drove much of that distance in silence. There were occasional spurts of superficial small talk, neither feeling strong enough to go beyond that. Eve attempted to initiate a conversation, but after several one-word replies, she gave up and turned the radio on, channel KRZA, public radio. The sun was in the western sky when they arrived.

The walls in Camilla's hospital room were an off-white color, clean and fresh, but devoid of color. There was no decoration and only a well-laundered, faded curtain separated her bed from the three others in the room. The room conveyed a sensitivity that reminded Eve of faded dreams. There was an undertone of bleach and chemicals rising from the well-scrubbed linoleum floor. At the far end of the room, there were windows in black metal frames, only openable at the top. Against this austere backdrop, there were live flowers of every color, cheerful drawings, and cards everywhere. The people in this room were loved.

Next to her bed was a whiteboard and scribbled in marker was the name of Camilla's nurse, Jeanne, and her medication schedule. Eve looked around at the IV stand with plastic saline bags, an LED heart monitor beeping in a low methodical pattern. She wanted nothing more than to run from the room.

Lying in the crisp, white sheets, still and silent was the woman that Eve loved more than any other person. Eve felt her heart splinter in her chest. A white-haired nurse checking vitals offered words of comfort to Eve and her father, before leaving them with the sleeping Camilla.

There she was, looking much like she had on the day that Eve left for college. The only visible differences were a few grey hairs and a quiet demeanor that was unlike anything Eve had experienced before. Even in sleep, Eve expected Camilla's smile that held the warmth of the sun. She ached for Camilla's larger than life personality, that both comforted and energized those around her, but today, Camilla lay motionless, expressionless.

Eve sat on the chair next to Camilla's bed and whispered into her ear, "Mom, it's your Evie, I'm home. Please wake up. We need you." She gently rubbed her arm and tears fell down her face. Once again, Eve felt broken. She thought back on the few times she experienced pain like this. Leaving her dolly bathing in the sun, her mother's unexpected departure, the first puppy she had to leave at the motel. She wondered whatever happened to him. The phone call from her father when she told them she was joining the FBI and he told her she was dead to him. Okay, Eve had to admit to herself that those were not his exact words. She had thought then that he was just being dramatic, that he would change his mind and things would go back to normal.

There was no response from Camilla. Her breathing was shallow and even her eyelids did not flutter, her hand remained limp in Eve's grasp. Eve's father left the room, saying something about coffee and the cafeteria. Eve opened the suitcase and pulled out one of the books, "Socialism and American Life." That book went back into the suitcase and out came "The Shadow of You." Eve knew this was a book authored by Camilla's friend, Brenda, and she sat back, opened the book, and started reading aloud while the older woman slept on.

Eve's dad returned with vending machine cups of coffee and sandwiches for them both. It was not Starbucks, or even Whole Bean coffee, but that didn't matter right now. She continued to read well into the night. When she was overcome by fatigue, she leaned forward and laid her head on the bed to be near Camilla. John was nearby asleep in an armchair.

They established a routine, each of them giving the other time to be alone with Camilla. The nurses would come in to check on the patient and the look on their faces increased Eve's sense of foreboding. The appearance of peaceful sleep was deceiving. Eve and John were both privately entertaining hopes of Camilla waking and returning home. Eve was quietly reading to Camilla and John was dozing in the chair when an alarm started wailing. The nurses rushed in and one forcefully escorted Eve and John to the waiting room.

Close to thirty minutes later, the doctor came out and shared with the small family that their beloved Camilla had passed. John held his little girl and they cried together, he wiped her green eyes with his soft, old, flannel shirt, and they walked hand-in-hand back to the hospital room. Together they said their goodbyes.

Camilla's family lived in Mexico and had not been able to get across the border to visit her in the hospital. Eve tasked herself with contacting her Abuela, Camilla's mother, to give her the terrible news. Camilla's Mexican family planned to apply for an emergency Visa and show up in the next day or two. After arranging with the hospital to transport Camilla to the Weylen's Funeral Home, John and Eve headed back to the house.

Eve could not imagine her father living without Camilla. She glanced over at the fragile-looking man and she knew she could not leave him without a plan in place to keep him sober and sane. By the time they made it back to the house, neighbors had already heard the news and were arriving with casseroles and condolences. Eve slipped away to update SAC Lange, then returned to the family room to reacquaint herself with old friends, and to meet new ones.

Within two days of Camilla's death, her family arrived from Mexico and were ready to prepare their Camilla in traditional Mexican fashion. Camilla was returned to her home, covered with a white sheet and placed on the floor, four lighted candles outlining a rectangular perimeter around her. For the next forty-eight hours, family and friends maintained a prayer vigil, including the children. During this time, visitors gathered in the home and Camilla's family made food and drinks for all who stopped by. At the end of the vigil, a coffin was delivered. Her family tenderly clothed her in a dress they had brought from Mexico and placed some of her favorite belongings inside the coffin with her.

After the funeral, the community wanted to do something special for the woman whom they considered one of the matriarchs of the village, and they arranged a potluck in her honor. When Eve arrived at the community center, the parking lot was filled with cars. When she walked inside, she realized that almost every one of the Tres Peidras residents was there to show their respect. Eve had never seen so many people in her little town together like this. She was convinced the population had doubled since she was last there and was unsure if the masses of people were known to her and simply older looking than she remembered or were complete strangers.

As Eve wandered from one small cluster of people to another, she listened to stories shared about Camilla and how she had so greatly affected the lives of her friends and neighbors. They also spoke passionately about the lack of affordable health care and how Camilla was not the first to die due to the inaccessibility of good health care. Camilla's insurance company had dropped her as soon as she was diagnosed with Diabetes Mellitus Type 2. As a long-term employed resident of NYC, Eve could not believe that Americans lived like that. The anger she felt was palpable. She knew she had to do something to honor Camilla and the love they shared.

Eve thought back on the philosophies that her father had so passionately espoused; the ideas that they were all equal and deserved the same treatment regardless of money and social status. Suddenly, these ideals became personal for Eve. It finally made sense to her, and she was determined to learn more over the next couple of days before she had to leave. She also knew she would have to maintain contact with her father, and provide him with purpose, so he could survive the pain.

Eve spent the remainder of her visit talking to her father about her life. She shared with him that the lack of relationships and children were personal choices. He, in turn, explained for the first time the real story behind what brought them to New Mexico so many years ago. The time they had together did not take away the pain, but it did rekindle a relationship that Eve and her father very much needed.

Knowing Eve worked for the Department of Justice

made her father hesitant to share what he was doing out in the bunker. Eve did not want to leave again without knowing what had occupied her father for so many years. She knew that if she could convince him that she would not turn him in, and that she would support him and his work, he might take her to his bunker. Sure enough, when Camilla's family had returned to Mexico, and it was just John, Eve, and Seba, he invited her down. When Eve had last seen the inside of the bunker, it had been an apocalypse prepper's dream. Now it looked like a situation room, a high-tech computer space with several layers of security. He told her about the technology and what it could do. John also revealed to Eve his username, BobD.

The level of trust that he showed Eve let her know that she was back in his good graces and whatever their future held; it would be the two of them against the world. She was captivated by his hacking skills and believed he was better than any FBI cyber specialist. John confided that his foundation in engineering gave him the edge. The way he saw the world, right down to pathways and code, was so abstract and mathematical, that a computer scientist, with no engineering acumen could not compare.

When it was time to go back to New York, Eve hoped her dad would be okay. They had agreed to a plan and that she would be back to check on him as soon as she could. Leaving this time was nothing like the mess she experienced when leaving for college. At that time, her father had refused to say goodbye, leaving Eve with overwhelming mixed emotions. She was torn between her desire to please her father versus the opportunity to go to college and live life like a normal person. The allure of normalcy won out. Evelyn Black had gone off to college and that was the last time she felt like daddy's green-eyed little girl.

As Eve prepared to return to Brooklyn, she gave her father a big hug and admitted she had taken something that belonged to him. She pulled from her bag the cotton flannel shirt that he had used to wipe her tears at the hospital. "Can I keep it, Daddy?"

He gave her a hug, "What is mine is yours." He said it with his own mixed emotions. Once again, she was leaving, and this time he would be without Camilla to distract him; this time he would be alone. The only saving grace was that he knew that this time they would remain close. They had made plans and he had to keep up his end of the bargain.

He managed to keep his composure until her jeep was down the road and out of sight. Then he broke down. John's chest ached. He felt a heaviness in his limbs and his body was cold. The world slowed down, his vision blurred, and he felt such despair that it threated to take him over. He reached his arm out to steady himself, using the table as a brace, then sat down, hunched over and cried. The tears soaked his sleeves. He knew life would never be the same, and for the first time in his life, he felt completely and utterly alone.

Losing Camilla was the hardest thing he had ever endured. Not even Eve's mother's sudden departure had hurt like this. When Alice had left him, he knew she was miserable. No matter how hard he had tried to make her happy, she continued to feel sorry for herself and detested her life with him as a fugitive. He had believed at the time that the birth of their little girl would help, but some women were not cut out to be mothers. With Camilla it was different, she loved him and Evie right down to her last breath.

His feelings for the two women were quite different. With Alice it was about passion. Beyond that, they had nothing in common until Evie came along. With Camilla, he shared an ideology, and their pillow talk was more exciting and meaningful than anything that he and Alice had shared. Camilla also wanted a daughter, and when she married John, she had one that she knew she could love and nurture like her own flesh and blood. It had been clear to Camilla that Evie needed a mother and Camilla had so much love to give.

Years prior, as soon as his bunker was Wi-Fi capable, John had tracked down Eve's mother. When he located her, Alice was living back in Michigan with her parents. A few years later, he saw her name back on the student list at the University of Michigan. He was glad to see she was finally going to finish her interior design degree.

He periodically found her at various stages of her life: her first design job after college, her marriage to a wealthy banker, and their subsequent children, Eve's two half-sisters and a half-brother. He saw a picture of the children and could see the resemblance. By now, all her half-siblings were professionals, earning six figures and achieving the American dream.

Not once had Alice ever made an attempt to find

him or their daughter. John knew that Eve had the same ability to find her mother as he had, but she never expressed an interest or need to do so. His thoughts drifted away from the past and back to his beautiful Camilla. What would his life be without her?

John and Seba walked out to the bunker. They took a few minutes to enjoy the open skies. The moon was so bright he could see for miles. John had to pick Seba up and carry him down the stairs. Seba was far too old to make it down the steep concrete steps. If John left him above, Seba would cry incessantly. He wouldn't be able to get any work done. He placed his dog on a soft blanket, pulled a bone out of his pocket to occupy him, and then sat down at his computer. He had work to do.

Chapter Four

It's All About Power

Evie had her first boyfriend in the sixth grade. His name was Karl. He and his mother lived at the SFH commune for a short time. Evie and Karl used to play together at the water tower across the street from her home. Karl was a pudgy little boy with sandy brown hair and a pronounced lisp. His biggest attribute was that he was a neighbor, his biggest fault was that he feared heights.

Evie tried to convince Karl to be adventurous, but he refused, until one sunny afternoon after a picnic lunch when she told Karl if he climbed to the top, she would grant him a kiss. That was the spark he needed, he grabbed ahold of the first rung and started climbing.

Several feet from the top Karl looked down, then tears started pouring from his eyes, and his breathing raced. His hands were sweaty, and he could not climb anymore.

Evie could not believe what a little baby he was. She was glad she wouldn't have to kiss him after all. "Just wait here, I will get help." Evie called up to Karl.

"No," he cried "Don't leave me Evie, I'm afraid."

She gave him a look, a blend of contempt at the boy's lack of courage, and fear of the trouble she would be in if he told on her.

"Hold on Karl, I have to get help." With that she ran off, ignoring his pleas."

Evie ran across the street to get Camilla, but before she made it, she heard a loud thud and she turned around. Karl was on the ground, one leg bent at an unusual angle and he was not crying anymore. "Bloody hell." Evie had heard that phrase once on the TV in town when she was with Camilla getting groceries. The heroine was ready to face danger, and she thought it to be the perfect expression for how she was feeling.

Evie repeatedly called for help. When Camilla appeared at the screen door and saw the motionless body on the ground, coupled with her stepdaughter's panicked look, she immediately called the ambulance. Dressed only in a house robe and slippers, Camilla raced across the street. When she was close enough to see that Karl was breathing, her body relaxed, and she sent Evie to fetch his mother. Evie raced to Karl's house and pounded on the door, yelling, "Mrs. P., Karl's hurt!"

It took what felt like forever for Mrs. P. to come to the door. She looked uncomprehendingly at Evie, and then over to Karl and Camilla by the tower. Karl's stout mother waddled as fast as she could, breathing heavily, over to Karl, crying, "My boy, my boy..."

Her questioning eyes begged Camilla for reassurance that her baby boy was going to be fine.

Camilla put her arm around the distraught woman and said, "Don't worry, Martha, he will be okay."

Shortly thereafter, the ambulance showed up and took both Karl and his mother away. After that event, he was no longer allowed to play with Evie and every time she saw his mother, she glowered at her. Evie was convinced Karl had told his mother about the bet and that the accident was her fault. Evie could not deny it. Losing a playmate should have troubled her, but the emotion that dominated was not one of sadness, but of power. Little Evie pondered the power that she had just wielded, persuading Karl to ignore his fears. It was her first taste of the strange satisfaction she found in manipulating others. It was not until much later that she realized the full impact of the situation. Karl could have died. She promised herself to never try that again.

She kept that promise until college. His name was Jim and was in her junior statistics class at Columbia. He showed up one night at 1020 when Eve was working. Eve thought he looked vaguely familiar but assumed she had just seen him around, perhaps at the bar. Winter semester was in full swing and Eve had to get some extra hours in to cover an unexpected hike in her heating bill. After Jim placed his order, she paid him very little attention, but she found herself glancing his direction from time and time. He was just so darn cute, like a puppy. He had a mop of messy hair and flashed her a big grin whenever he caught her eye. Eve could not help but smile herself. At some point in the evening, when she looked over in his direction, the young man was gone.

The next evening, back at work, he showed up again. This time, she spoke to him. Eve had to raise her voice to speak over the music, chatter of nearby patrons, and the usual clatter one made when bartending. She started with a "Hey there, you're back." But she said it in such a way that it sounded like a question.

He grinned at her so wide she saw all of his white teeth and thought to herself what great dental hygiene he must have. Then, realizing how weird that observation seemed, she was relieved she had not said it aloud. "I'm like one of those silly girls I hate so much," she told herself, and turned attention to another patron.

He interrupted her train of thought and said, "Yes, I'm back, I guess I just enjoyed this drink," he looked down at the drink again, and back up at her, "What is this called again?"

"An Old Fashioned," she told him.

"Ah, yes, the Old Fashioned," he drank it down in one gulp, "I'm here for that." He paused, trying to think of something else to say, "What's in it?"

Eve was just looking at him, this amusing guy that just tossed back his drink. If he kept that up, she would be getting him a cab. "1 1/2 oz bourbon whiskey, 2 dashes angostura bitters, 1 sugar cube, and a few dashes plain water, you should ease up a bit on the drinking, it can hit you hard."

"Alrighty then, what do you suggest I have next?"

Seriously, who uses the word, 'alrighty'? Instead of asking him, she said, "Maybe a glass of water?"

"Okay then, a glass of water please, young lady," and tipped his imaginary hat.

"We're probably the same age." she said, once again raising her voice to be heard over the bar.

Jim slid out of his seat and moved down to be closer to her, "So you don't have to yell. I'm twenty-one, how old are you?"

"The same, where are you from?" Eve asked him, she was very curious about his accent and easy-going demeanor.

"Clinton, Iowa, right on the mighty Mississippi! Don't you think you should ask me my name before asking such personal questions?" He then gave her a smile and a half-wink that said he was teasing her.

"That explains so much!" she thought, but what she said was, "Okay, what's your name?"

"My name is Jim, it's very nice to meet you, Eve."

The use of her name startled her. She knew she had not given it, and she certainly did not wear a name tag. She stood up rigid, furrowed her eyebrows and pursed her lips and stared at him. She started to say something, when he interrupted, "Relax, we're in the same statistics class with Dr. Greshner, I sit two seats behind you on the left."

Eve did relax. The sudden tension across her shoulders lifted, "Oh, yeah, that's right; I thought you looked familiar."

The two continued with small talk and banter throughout the evening, and shortly before she had to close, he told her goodnight.

The next day in class Eve saw him there, sitting right where he said he would be, when she walked through the door. She touched his shoulder as she passed by and offered up a good morning. Jim responded in kind and she continued to her seat.

That evening at work Eve kept looking over at the door, expecting Jim to show up, he never did. He was also not in class; she was a little worried. It was a week before she saw him again.

When he did turn up at the bar, he was not quite himself. Now, Eve knew she did not know him very well, but she noticed his spark was gone. He gave her a weak smile when he sat down, and she rushed to give him his Old Fashioned. He took it and murmured a shallow thank you. After three more rounds, and about the same amount of communication, Eve could not take it anymore.

"What's wrong with you? You haven't been to class, and you look so miserable." She was trying to be gentle, but it wasn't really her thing. Eve came across more abrupt and matter of fact.

Jim looked up at her, with sad glossy eyes, "My father died, I had to go back home and take care of things."

Eve looked up at the clock, "I have an hour until I'm off, stay here, and when I'm done, we'll talk."

He agreed to stay and asked for another round. Three was more than his normal, and a fourth would likely leave him a little drunk, but she could handle it. She brought him another drink, this one weaker than the previous three.

When her shift was finally over, she grabbed a hold of Jim's arm with one hand, and his drink in the other, and said "Let's go over there." She pointed to a far corner, and off they went. Eve did not drink often; she had spent too many nights watching people drink too much and become complete fools. She wanted no part of such behaviors.

Eve sat across from him and just looked him over. Jim was a soft spoken, slender man with geeky, retro glasses that hid amazing blue eyes. He was quite good-looking but did not seem to realize it. Their conversation was a little forced until they got onto the topic of music. They both liked music from the 70s and some of the less commercial stuff of the 80s, but as far as the 90s were concerned, there was little worth mentioning.

At the end of the night, Jim offered to take Eve home, for her safety. Eve nearly scoffed. Her father and the others at SFH made sure she could take care of herself, so she knew very little fear. That did not stop her from allowing Jim to escort her home. She knew he could benefit from a sober companion, and likely needed someone around to keep his mind off his father.

During the walk home together, Jim spoke about his life back in Clinton, Iowa. He told Eve how difficult moving to New York had been. He could tell right away that she felt as out of place as he did. Jim admitted he had heard she worked at the bar and showed up hoping to get a chance to speak with her. Eve wasn't sure if she liked that. By the time they made it back to her apartment it was near three in the morning. Eve knew no sane person should be out at this hour, especially in her neighborhood. Central Park can be dangerous after hours.

Eve lived in an Upper West Side apartment complete with exposed brick walls, and New York's version of a spacious bedroom, which, in any other city, would be considered a closet. The fact that it was a separate room made it worth more than a standard studio apartment. It was the proximity to the school, the hardwood floors, and brick walls that sold her on the place. She tucked Jim in on the sofa, with pillows, blankets, a few aspirin, and a huge bottle of water.

She woke the next morning expecting to find him fast asleep, but he was, in fact, gone. Eve was concerned for about a minute, then shrugged her shoulders, and hopped in the shower. By the time she was out and drying off there was a knock on the door. It was Jim, with coffee and donuts. Coffee and donuts, what did she do to deserve this? Eve was freaking ecstatic; she loved coffee and donuts. No one had ever done this before.

They sat together and enjoyed breakfast. Eve ending up wearing raspberry filling on her face and shirt, but she didn't give it a thought. Jim, however, smiled, reached up with a napkin, and wiped a bit of jelly from the corner of her mouth. Eve could not stop smiling. It was in her eyes, in her body language, and stayed there all the way to class. Jim offered to carry her books, but she politely declined, a girl had limits after all.

Jim did not show up at the bar that night but did make another appearance the next morning. He had a bag of goodies and coffee in hand. He stood smiling at her when she opened the door. Eve grabbed the bag and looked inside, scrunched up her face and drew in a deep breath through her nose, "What's this?" She asked. Whatever it was it smelled heavenly, and she had no plans to turn it down. He laughed and pulled out two big rolls stuffed with eggs, sausage, cheese, and hot sauce.

"Hot Sauce?" Eve queried.

"Well, you did say your mother was Mexican, so I thought you wouldn't mind a bit of heat."

"No no no, I don't mind at all, it's lovely, I've just never had something like this. The bread, is it a roll, a bun...?"

"It's something my mother used to make us before school. The bread is made from corn and is wrapped around the egg/cheese/sausage mixture and baked. Then, of course, we dip it in ketchup, hot sauce, or eat it plain. It depended on how much of a hurry we were in."

Eve took a big bite, cheese oozing down her chin, "It's so freaking good, Jim, where did you buy 'em?"

"I didn't, I made 'em. The other night you were talking about how much you missed your stepmom and her home cooking. I knew I had to make this for you, so last night I went shopping, and prepped them. Then today I got up early to make them in the dorm kitchen." He tipped his paper cup, "But the coffee I bought."

Eve leaned over and gave him a kiss on the cheek. This was the first romantic-ish gesture between them. Jim's cheeks reddened, but he didn't let that stop him, he returned the kiss, but this time on her mouth. They headed to class, and about a block into the walk Jim reached out and slid his fingers into hers. No words were spoken; they just continued to walk.

It was not long before Jim was spending every evening with Eve at her place or hanging out with her at the bar. He did schoolwork while she tended the bar, and, when possible, he helped her with her schoolwork. She did not need the help. There was just not enough time in the day for her to go to class, work full time, and keep up with homework, which was what her bills required. Jim continued to treat her every morning to coffee and some breakfast treats. On her days off, he would cook for the both of them at her place. Jim was always thinking of her and bringing her silly gifts, like a cactus plant so she wouldn't miss home so much. Then, of course, he had to insist she let him care for it when he saw her drowning the poor plant with a cup of water nearly every day.

Eve knew it was silly to make him leave after a wonderful dinner, knowing he would show up again first thing in the morning, but the idea of having a man stay the night, was unknown territory and frankly a little overwhelming. She knew this routine could not continue so she finally bit the bullet and asked him to stay the night. The rest of that evening was fraught with awkwardness. Where should he sleep, he didn't have pajamas, or even a toothbrush with him. He could tell she was nervous, and also knew that she was far too proud to admit it, so as the evening wore on, he politely backed out. He told her that next time they had evening plans, he would pack an overnight bag and he would stay the night.

It finally happened, he brought a bag, and a guitar, and they made an occasion of it. That night, after a bottle of wine, and some rather spectacular guitar playing, he stayed. They had a night neither one of them would forget. Over breakfast the next morning she commented on his outstanding guitar playing and asked why he didn't do it professionally. He admitted he did not like to play in front of others. She thought this was a little silly and told him so. His feelings were hurt, and they didn't speak to one another on the way to class.

Eve knew she had been harsh. She did not like people in general and no one ever called her out on it. Why did she have to make Jim feel bad? She thought about his fear of singing in public, and then her mind went back to Karl and the water tower. She decided she would help Jim overcome his fears. First, she had to undo the damage she had done.

Jim had no problem forgiving Eve, he was head over heels in love with her. It was not long before he was staying every night at her place, and they had a perfect relationship, or so he thought.

Unlike with Karl and his fall from the tower, Eve was going to be more intentional and methodical in her goal to rid Jim of his fears. She would eventually have Jim performing in public and he would think it was his idea. This time she worked slowly. The weather was improving, so she suggested a picnic at central park and pleaded with him to bring his guitar. They ate sandwiches, drank lemonade, and finally he pulled it out. There were very few people around. New York was still rather chilly in April. He played a few songs, before putting it away. Then they would lay on the blanket and she told him stories about life in the desert.

Saturdays in the park with Jim continued well into May, and the small crowds began to gather to hear Jim play. It was not long before Jim was playing in front of five, ten... twenty people. It seemed his fear was gone, until the day when Eve suggested he play at the bar.

Jim was already in a mood. His mother was calling his cell. In fact, she did this several times a day which Eve found very annoying, but Jim took it in stride. Since his father's death Jim had stepped up and helped his mother with some financial questions. He promised to take a closer look at it when he returned home. When Eve suggested playing at the bar Jim visibly recoiled, and responded with a firm no.

Eve was frustrated, convincing Karl to climb the tower had been soooo much easier. Jim's aversion to public performance made him less in her eyes. The next evening Jim told her he had to go to Iowa for a few days and asked Eve to join him. It was her turn to recoil. The idea of going with him to meet his family was as upsetting to her as the idea of playing in public was to him.

After much thought she decided to make a proposition, "You play in the bar, and I," and she almost choked on this, "will go to Iowa with you." After some voicing several objections, and a few shots of something alcoholic Eve had laying around, he reluctantly agreed.

That evening he showed up at the bar. Eve had made all the arrangements and the stage was ready for him but was he ready for the stage? Minutes before it was time, Jim got so nervous he rushed into the men's room to vomit, twice. It was a weeknight so there were very few people there. This helped a lot. Eve reminded him that he had more people showing up in the park than there were in the audience. He finally built up enough courage and walked up onto the stage and sat in the chair. The lights were bright, and he felt the need to close his eyes for a few seconds until they adjusted, but then looked down at his fingers and started to play. He didn't look up again until he was nearly done with the first song. When he saw all the smiles on the faces, no one laughing, or looking ready to boo him off the stage, he relaxed. The burst of applause when he finished the song gave him an unexpected rush. Jim kept playing for another forty-five minutes.

The audience did not just clap, they stood and clapped and called for an encore. Jim could not believe it; his euphoria was something he never knew he could feel. He looked over at Eve, behind the bar, glass in hand and towel in another, smiled and mouthed a "Thank you." He also noticed a young woman who looked familiar in the front near the stage. She had lovely long brown hair, and a green dress.

Several of the audience members walked over to speak to Jim personally after the set. They told him how great he played and offered to buy him drinks. The green dress girl waited patiently for an opportunity to talk to him. Her name was Wendy, and she asked him when he would be playing again. Jim looked over at Eve. Eve shrugged, as if to say, "It's up to you." He turned back to Wendy and said, "I'll be back tomorrow."

Jim continued to play for the bar, and Wendy of the green dress continued to show up and watch. Eve knew she should be feeling jealousy, or something like it, but she was getting tired. She had no time to herself, and all of her energy was divided between work, school, and Jim. It was draining. Besides, his showing up at the bar every night was costing her money. No one wanted to tip a girl with her boy-friend nearby. When Eve suggested he not show up every night Jim's feelings were so hurt she felt like the biggest bitch alive.

For Eve the thrill was over, Jim was now playing regularly, and she wanted her life back. The semester was ending and the trip to Iowa was scheduled for the upcoming weekend. She knew she couldn't do it. After class the next day Eve told him she couldn't see him anymore. Between work and classes, she didn't have time for the relationship. He didn't take it well. He cried and told her how much he loved her. With grow-ing impatience, Eve outwardly expressed sadness and regret. She assured him he was wonderful, and she was sorry to hurt him. She gave him a final hug and slipped a piece of paper into his hand, and walked away. When she disappeared from view, Jim opened the paper and found the simple clean, structured font which he knew to be Eve's handwriting, Wendy's name and number, followed by "She's for you, Jim. Call her."

He gave a small laugh at the curt note. He thought for a moment, pictured the way Wendy of the green dress looked at him. She had been there to see him play several times since that first night. They hadn't really talked much, but when she did speak to him, her face lit up. She stood out in the bar crowd, but it wasn't necessarily her beauty. It was more like an aura of innocence. Maybe Eve was right. Wendy was the kind of girl he could take home to Iowa, a rarity in New York City. His anger at Eve slid away, and he found himself looking forward to seeing his new fan again.

Having her apartment back to herself felt like a vacation to Eve. She couldn't believe that she had allowed Jim to practically live with her for nearly five months. It was another ten months before she considered another relationship.

Her name was Judy. Eve met Judy one day at the library. They struck up a conversation and Eve asked her to lunch. Judy was attractive in a very athletic, prep school way, with short light brown hair, natural blond highlights, high cheekbones, and a long neck. She reminded Eve of a Gap boy model. Eve could tell right away that Judy was attracted to her, but she was sure that even if Judy were aware of her own feelings, she would never act on them. Judy came from an upbringing that frowned upon the homosexual way of life. Her denial was so deep she had never acknowledged her own sexual ambiguity.

Eve had a new mission (as she had begun to call them), "Get the Girl out of the Closet." She had dubbed her time with Jim as "Guitar Boy Gone Wild." She took copious notes on her subjects and her observations, locking them away to make sure they would never be seen by anyone. She knew these experiments would not be seen as anything other than the manipulation of others. Eve saw it quite differently, but she had known early on that her thought processes were not like others. In her notes she wrote, "It is my belief that humans are emotional creatures, far too emotional, and this stops them from being productive, getting ahead, and is a liability." She continued, "Caring can be a crutch and causes people to make poor decisions. Subject #1 was so worried that he would look foolish in front of others. He displayed fight or flight activation at the mere mention of playing his guitar in public." Eve was quite methodical in her notetaking, she kept track of times, dates, weather, and people with which they interacted. She tracked the daily activities of her subjects and the people in the spheres.

The meetings with Judy continued. They met every Saturday in the library and shared late lunches in the afternoon. Then, on one lovely spring day, Eve suggested they go for a walk at Morningside Park.

At one point along the walk, Eve pretended to stumble, and Judy caught her. Eve thought to herself, "Humans are predictable creatures." They spent several seconds in close contact before they disconnected from the almost embrace. The next time they saw one another, Judy had suggested they go to the movies. They arrived together like good friends, but by the end of the movie, they looked like something more. The two took advantage of any opportunity to touch, hold hands, and sat so close their arms were almost intertwined.

One day they took it a bit further. They had spent the day hiking and ended up back at Eve's place. Eve made them a salad while Judy showered, then Judy prepared the pasta while Eve took her turn. When dinner was ready, they sat down at the thrift store table, on oak Windsor chairs, and shared a bottle of wine. When the bottle of wine was empty, Eve leaned over and kissed Judy. Judy did not pull away. She returned the kiss and they looked into each other's eyes. Without a word exchanged, they understood one another and left the last few bites of dinner on their plates. They turned up the music, washed the dishes, and cleaned up the kitchen. They sang along with the music and lightly touched one another in passing while they worked. That night Eve and Judy shared the bed, and before they fell asleep Judy whispered in Eve's ear, "With you I can do anything, be anyone." Eve held her breath, "Please don't say you love me, please don't say you love me," over and over in her head. When those words did not pass Judy's lips, Eve relaxed and soon fell asleep with Judy's head on her chest.

Soon they were walking around campus openly hand-in-hand and joined the Columbia Pride club. Judy started dressing in more and more masculine outfits and began referring to herself as Jude. Many of the femme girls crushed on Judy, but Judy only had eyes for Eve.

The experiment was over. Eve had achieved her goal and just in time too. Eve selected one of the more attractive women in the pride club and groomed an attraction between her and Jude. Jude had become who she needed to be. Eve had pushed her to be the person she knew Judy had held deep inside. She had taken her out of her comfort zone and was leaving her in good hands. When Eve tried to explain this to her, Judy took it quite well. Or at least in front of Eve she did. There were a few tears and a lengthy hug, but all in all, the termination of the mission went smoothly, or so she stated in her journal.

That night, Eve went back to her place very pleased with her ability to recognize what people want and help them achieve their hidden desires. Perhaps her methods were not the most scientific, and a few hearts may have been broken along the way, but Eve felt that, on balance, the long-term benefit to the subjects was more important.

The best class she had in college was her Psychology of Leadership course. The professor teaching the class was young. It was his first position after finishing up his post-doctorate at Yale. Dr. Alistair FitzHerbert was originally from Norbury, Derbyshire, in England. Rumors were that his father was a Baron, but in all likelihood, she thought, it was just a rumor. What were the chances a Baron's son would be teaching at Columbia? Apparently, as she would soon find out, quite good.

On the first day of class Dr. FitzHerbert instructed the students to call him Alistair, or Al. Eve took one look at his British country gentleman attire and knew there was no chance in hell she could call this guy Al, so Alistair it was. Eve could not believe how well his class fit her needs. He shared with them all the tricks to win people over, to take over a meeting, to hijack a conversation, to identify verbal and nonverbal cues and to feign interest or convincingly display other emotions. What he offered in his class was everything that made Eve want to study Psychology. Rather than discouraging the desire for power and control, he was essentially teaching the class how to gain and embrace it.

Every week it was something new, and when the semester was over, she continued to meet with Alistair and pepper him with questions. She felt for the first time she could be honest about her desire to manipulate others and that the drive to do so was the reason behind her pursuit of a degree in Psychology. Rather than being repelled by this information, he seemed to appreciate it.

He had never met anyone like Eve, someone that seemed to be a female version of himself. Alistair was the younger of two sons and it was his elder brother that would inherit his father's title. Alistair wanted power and control. He was determined to demonstrate to his father that, in spite of the fact that he was ineligible to inherit the family title, he was, in fact, more worthy than his elder brother.

Alistair had studied hard and been accepted into the best schools the United States had to offer. This was not enough for his father, who found psychology an unacceptable field of study. According to him, it was pseudoscience and only broken people would consider the field. They must have a need to try to fix themselves. "Go be a doctor, a lawyer, something respectable for God's sake."

When Alistair graduated with his Ph.D., his father did not even bother to show up. When he received a faculty position at Columbia, his father sent a handwritten letter congratulating him.

Eve and Alistair were so alike that they bonded more as brother and sister than they did as girlfriend and boyfriend. When Eve was no longer his student, the two would attend parties together. At the start of the evening, they would challenge each other to a little competition to occupy their time. Typically, they would find the most arrogant person in the room and topple him/her in front of his/her friends or colleagues.

One evening, at a bar, they had been playing their little game. A young student from Columbia was showing off, sharing what was likely something about finance that he had learned just that morning in class, but attempting to make it sound like insider gossip from Wall Street. Alistair pointed out the flaw in the kid's logic. Alistair was a psychologist, but the man knew a thing or two about money. Eve was glad he had drawn the short straw this night, she could not have bested the student nearly as well as Allister.

Reflecting back on when the evening went wrong, and remembering every detail was difficult. She remembered the guy boasting about the interest rates and how the poor had no concept of money and it was their lack of knowledge that kept them down. This economic philosophy was offensive to many in the bar. The place appeared to have a mixed crowd but leaned heavier on the side for the wealthy rather than the poor.

"They deserve their lot in life, they have no mind for

anything above minimum wages, be it in labor, retail, or cleaning my toilets." His friends laughed. A few patrons within earshot heard the drunken statements, stood up and walked out.

Alistair spoke up, asking the student how much he made an hour. The student, taken aback at the question said with authority, "I do not work." As if the mere idea was beneath him.

"So," Alistair commented, "You, an unemployed young punk, living off your parents, I presume, feel worthy to put down people that work for a living; people who do not have the opportunities you have, like college and well-to-do-parents. You feel that you are somehow better than these people; Do I have this right?"

The young man stuttered a bit, "I did not say I was better."

"Oh, I beg to differ, young man, you most certainly did, and you said they did not deserve the same things you do. Why do you think you deserve more? Because of Mommy and Daddy? You are a pathetic, entitled, little boy and deserve nothing."

The crowd applauded. The kid's face reddened, and he looked like he wanted to hurt someone, most likely Alistair. Eve suggested they pay the bill and leave, and when Alistair set out to do so he found out his bill had already been paid. When he asked by whom, an older man walked up to him and shook his hand and said, "I paid your bill, you made me proud. I can tell from your clothes and manner of speech that you come from wealth. I just wanted to say how impressed I am that you stood up to that idiot and supported those less fortunate. Sadly, that doesn't happen enough in this day and age." Alistair thanked the man and they left.

The short exchange had cost them some time and when they took off in their car, they realized the entitled boy, who had been humiliated by their game, was following them. He was driving all over the road, clearly intoxicated. Alistair wanted to pull over, but Eve was convinced the guy was the kind of person who would have a gun, a bat, or some form of weapon. She encouraged Alistair to speed up. They were on NY9A and a dense fog lingered over the highway. Fortunately, there were few cars on the road. The moonlight did little to improve visibility. Eve looked behind them. Entitled-boy was still behind them, and driving as recklessly as ever. When they were getting off the exit near the pier, they heard a crash. Entitled-boy's car did not slow down enough to make the exit and ended up on the Hudson River Greenway, upside down. Smoke was rising from the overturned car and small flames were licking at the engine. Alistair stopped his car and started to get out. Eve pulled him back, "Alistair, you can't. You've been drinking and if the cops test you, you could be charged with driving under the influence. Think about it! I am still a student. Your career would be over." He paused for a moment, staring at the flames, then sat back down, closed the door, and drove off, very slowly.

When they got to Eve's place, he dropped her off at the curb and left without a word. That was the last time she saw him. She heard that he took a leave of absence and went back to his home in England. Eve had checked the newspapers the next day looking for something about the crash, but she was never able to find anything. She chose to believe that someone had stopped and pulled him out in time to save him, and that he must be in a hospital somewhere. Maybe he was even safe at home.

Eve became increasingly convinced that dating and/or relationships were not for her. People close to her experienced mental or physical damage, and she knew she was to blame. When she reflected on her own emotions, she realized she had none. She did not feel regret, sorrow, or remorse. This was the second time in her life that she thought something inside her must be broken. She could not pinpoint when she had become like this; if there was just one incident, perhaps her mother leaving?

It had been a long time since she had thought about her mother. She cared so little about Eve and so much about herself, that she left her little girl and never looked back. Maybe her mother was broken too, maybe she lacked emotions just as Eve did. Maybe that was why Eve had such difficulty feeling. How else could a mother leave a child that way. She found this a strangely comforting explanation for her abandonment.

Eve had looked up her mother once in the library. A librarian showed her how to use the microfiche index and Eve spent a few afternoons looking at newspapers from her mother's hometown, looking for clues as to what happened to her. Eve wasn't able to find anything. She wasn't sure if this was good or bad but thought likely both.

Eve had given up on relationships and focused on her schoolwork. She even quit her job at 1020 and took a position as a librarian assistant at the New York Public Library. During her senior year she attended a job fair. The FBI had a table. Eve found a seat and started to think. The FBI, she could use her skills in psychology and solve cases. Her ability to mimic others and to blend in would also help. Carrying a gun would be pretty cool too. But could she really do it? Her father, Eve thought about her father. She almost tabled the idea right then and there. "But it's been years since the feds showed up at Tres Piedras, surely, he would be okay with this decision."

She could at least talk to the FBI recruiters, find out how to apply. Ignoring all the other tables, she walked right up to the FBI table where two individuals sat, and said, "I want to know more, please." Thirty minutes later she was enrolled in the FBI Honors internship program and from there she went straight into the FBI.

Telling her father she was joining the FBI was something Eve was dreading. She knew he would not take it well, so she first tried it out on Camilla. The call went something like, "Mom, I am joining the FBI." Pause, longer pause, time dragged until Camilla responded with... "That's great Evie." She had never stopped calling her that, and it was around the age of thirteen when Eve transitioned from Camilla to Mom. Eve knew that Camilla was just as hesitant to tell John as she herself was.

Camilla asked if Eve had been accepted. If there was a chance that she would not be going, why burden John with the news?

"Yes," Eve told her, "I have been accepted and start next month." Camilla and John knew Eve had been in a special honors program, but Eve had not told them that is was a Department of Justice, FBI sponsored program.

The two spent several minutes debating whether or not to tell John at this exact moment, or put it off for maybe a day, a week, several years... they both agreed tearing the Band-Aid off fast was the best solution, so Camilla called John to the phone. He took the phone, a smile on his face and said, "Hi, baby, what's up?"

Eve wanted to back out, but it was too late. "Dad, I've decided to join the FBI."

The following pause lasted forever. "What? Why? How could you?" That's all she heard.

"Daddy, let me explain, my degree..."

And that was all he let her say before he interrupted. "Eve, you know what this means, if you do this, we have to sever ties. There is no other solution."

"But Daddy, you have a different name, you're not the man you were back then, besides, I don't believe anyone is still looking for you, I doubt you were that wanted." She was starting to get a little upset, it was her dream, and he was crushing it.

"It is understandable that you do not know the repercussions of what you are saying, perhaps I shielded you too much from the truth, but honestly, Eve, have you no sense?"

At this she was very offended, and most definitely her father's daughter, "Daddy, this is what I am going to do, if you can't support me, I don't know what else there is to say." And like a petulant child she hung up. That was the last conversation they had, until the call to come home, several years later.

Chapter Five

Preparation

The FBI hired a style coach to get her ready for her unique undercover assignment. The purpose was not only to wipe out any characteristics Eve possessed that would call her out as an FBI agent, but to give her a persona that would make men want to talk to her, to get to know her. Then Eve, in turn, could get to know them. Eve balked at the idea that she needed a coach. She believed she could go undercover without the help from style experts. It's not like she didn't take care of herself. Her hair was clean and healthy, her clothes, while not name brand, fit well. She did admit that her wardrobe consisted only of three black suits, two with pants and one with a pencil skirt, five white oxford cotton shirts, two sweaters, one navy and one gray, and several pairs of "Quantico" workout sweats and tees. Okay, so maybe her wardrobe could be improved, by why spend so much money?

Kohls, Macy's, and Amazon suited her just fine. Amazon shopping, with the ability to shop without bumping into people or having small talk with the cashier, could not get any better. Kohls, she could not believe was even on her list of acceptable stores. The cashier small talk included five minutes of trying to convince her to get the store credit card, every-single-time. Macy's was not much better. She might truly enjoy shopping if self-checkout was an option everywhere.

When the style coach showed up at her desk, Eve was engrossed in her stack of background data on the proposed terrorists and arms dealers that were likely to be showing up at this clandestine IDEC. The style coach coughed, daintily, and when Eve spun her swivel chair around, she found herself looking up at one of the tallest women she had ever seen.

When Eve stood, she reached the woman's shoulders. Eve was not a short woman, at 5 foot 7, and more often than not, she found herself taller than most of the females she encountered She liked it that way. The coach had to be over six foot tall. Eve admitted to herself that she felt a little intimidated. Just the fact she had to look up at this woman made her incredibly uncomfortable and angry. Her discomfort was only slightly relieved when she realized the woman was wearing four-inch heels and was not actually as tall as she seemed. "Bloody hell," she thought to herself, but to the Amazon she said, "So, you're here to turn me into something like you?"

Samantha responded, "I'm not here to make you into me, that could never happen, but what I will do is convince others that you know a thing or two about style. I want you to accomplish this mission without embarrassing me, nor being identified as an FBI agent." She said it without condemnation or smile, which, damn it, made her even more intimidating. Samantha turned toward the door.

It never occurred to Eve until this very minute how a well-dressed woman could use her sense of style in such a powerful way. She was not about to let this woman know that she found her intimidating. She looked skeptically at Samantha's feet. "I hope you can walk in those shoes."

Samantha abruptly stopped, turned to Eve and said "Walk? That's not happening. We're taking my car."

Eve, feeling a little confused about taking a car to get to a store a mile away, said, "We'll be lucky to find parking any closer than where we are now."

"We will not be concerning ourselves with parking," Samantha replied in a matter of fact way. When the two ladies stepped outside, a beautiful red Mercedes Maybach was waiting, complete with a chauffeur holding the car door open.

The chauffeur wore a driving cap, a plain, collared, white dress shirt with a black tie, and a matching black suit jacket and pants. The jacket and pants were simple, no unusual piping, decorations, or designs.

To complete the look, he had on polished black dress shoes and driving gloves.

They were barely out of the parking spot when Eve yelled up to the driver, "Take Barkley, Reade Street is at a dead stop this time of day."

Samantha, without even glancing at her, quietly stated, "This is not a taxi, he knows what he is doing."

Eve sat back in the seat and with what some would call a pout on her face. Samantha looked calmly excited, "We can make it to Saks, Salvatore Ferragamo, Burberry for a nice set of luggage, Tory Burch, Gucci, and then lunch at L'Appart." The very thought of going to so many stores already exhausted Eve, and they were not yet at the first.

Samantha had arranged a personal shopper to be waiting for them when they arrived at Saks. Eve started wishing she could have required hazard pay for this assignment. The shopper took a glance at Eve's off-the-rack black suit and what may once have been a crisp white shirt. A look of disgust briefly passed across her perfectly contoured face.

When Eve reached out to shake hands with the personal shopper, the woman stepped back, as if she felt Eve's poor fashion sense was contagious. The shopper tried to cover up her reaction, reminded herself she was a professional, and with a big bright smile that framed her too-white teeth, she took Eve's hand warmly and said with precise enthusiasm, "We are going to have so much fun." She then proceeded to address only Samantha for the rest of the Saks experience, as if Eve was a young child not worthy of her time.

Samantha and the personal shopper quickly became the best of friends. The shopper held up a beautiful ivory/pink floral print wrap dress with crochet trim details, short sleeves, and side tie closure "Samantha, what do you think about this dress on her?" After a quick glance at Eve, she responded with a nod of approval.

After a few more choice outfits, they ended up in the shoe area. Even though Eve knew she was in the hands of a professional, she had to interject, "Who in their right mind would spend $700 on a pair of shoes just because they have red soles?" The two ladies just looked at Eve with pity. Eve never thought to ask if she was able to keep the spoils of this mission, the clothes, the shoes, and especially the upcoming luggage, which, she was sure, would be quite lovely. Clothes can tighten and go out of style, but luggage will always fit, as would shoes and jewelry.

By the time they shuttled her off to the dressing room, she had three sales assistants carrying clothes, shoes, and intimates. The last bit being something she had no idea why she needed, nor was she willing to model for the Saks staff. When Samantha saw Eve in one of the dresses, she commented on its effortless wrap style, and that it was an intensely feminine dress with a near liquid drape. When they encouraged Eve to walk, they all complimented the dress's beautiful movement, the deep hem flounce, and ruffle-detailed bodice. This was all so foreign to Eve, but she had to admit, she looked good. It was when the camera came out, and photos were taken for each outfit, that she started to feel uncomfortable again.

The next step, Burberry. Eve was happy they were only there to buy luggage, and when she saw the $2000.00 price tag for one piece, she decided to not look at prices for the rest of the day. She thought wryly that the FBI's confiscated drug money was being put to dubious use. Tory Burch and Gucci were not so bad. The stores were small enough to make the shopping fast. Eve was now accustomed to the looks of disdain from the sales ladies and found it easy to ignore them.

Lunch, on the other hand, was a bit more complex. She had hoped they could go to Benares for Indian Cuisine, but Samantha insisted on going French. L'Appart was an exclusive, apartment-like restaurant. According to Samantha, the tasting menu was divine, and no one understood French desserts like chef Abello.

The last part of this Miss Congeniality makeover was to go to the Marie Robinson Salon to get tweezed and blown and whatever other medieval torture Frédérique chose to use on her. The makeover included makeup application lessons. The brushes and wands felt foreign in Eve's unpracticed hands. Frédérique and Samantha exchanged looks over her head as he corrected her blush placement and tsk-tsked about the mess she made with the finishing powder. A bag of much-needed accessories and products finished off the shopping experience for the day.

Before the driver dropped her off back at the office, Samantha made it clear that Eve was to start the beauty regime the very next day. "We have to make you look like you were born to wear these clothes, and that will only happen with practice."

She knew Samantha was right. On her way back home, she stopped at Grimaldi's. They had the best pizza pie in Brooklyn. Later that evening, Eve walked around the apartment in her new Christian Louboutin shoes, wearing only her t-shirt and boxers, a slice of greasy pizza in hand, listening to Nina Simone via Bluetooth speakers.

The next morning, she woke up an hour early. After she spent an ungodly amount of time on her hair and makeup, she put on one of the new dresses, selected matching shoes, and headed off to her favorite coffee shop. As soon as she walked into the shop, she pasted on a smile that she believed matched her outfit. The familiar smells of the coffee blends, the chatter of the customers, and the churning of the espresso machines instantly relaxed her.

When it was her turn to order she asked for a unicorn Frappuccino, then off she went to stand in line with the other fancy-coffee-drinkers. Eve felt very proud of herself. She even struck up a conversation with the gentlemen behind her. The barista called her name. Eve picked up the pink drink and took a sip. The taste surprised and repulsed her so much that she dropped the cup. The slush launched from the cup like a waterspout, landing on her new clothes, the floor, and the man behind her. She looked up in bewilderment at the baristas behind the counter, all of which clambered to help her, then she glanced back at the man trying to clean off his jacket with about twenty recycled brown paper napkins. Eve dashed out of the shop. She paused a block away to look down at her front and the pink mess. She decided it almost blended into the pink flowers of the wrap dress.

She headed off to the office without her morning caffeine and the scowl on her face kept everyone away. When Samantha showed up, binder in hand, Eve tensed, concerned about what she might have to say. Samantha took one look at Eve with the unicorn frap mess on her dress and marched straight into the boss's office.

"Eve get in here," said her SAC with a voice not used to being denied. Eve walked in and stood in front of his desk next to Samantha. He took one look at Eve and his first thought was wow, was this really the young agent that caused him so much frustration? The large pink stain over the front of the dress and the look on her face made him laugh from the gut so loudly, that all the agents in the vicinity looked curiously through the glass walls.

Samantha looked annoyed and started to say something. Eve expected a berating about being a heathen and not worthy of her time, but what she said was, "I will fetch her another dress." With the click clack of her heels, she stalked out of the room. Eve went back to her desk and immersed herself in the stacks of files. Samantha returned twenty minutes later with a dress matching the one she was wearing and said, "Change."

Eve went off to the bathroom, changed her dress and when she returned, she handed the damaged frock to Samantha.

"Please, be more careful with this one, Eve," Samantha admonished and returned to SAC Lange's office, closing the door.

Chapter Six

New Identity

For most people, Eve included, cell phones are self-imposed prosthetics, and their lives are profoundly impaired if the battery is dead, or worse yet, if the phone is lost. Eve had a high level of respect for computer types. The juxtaposition of their confidence in their work and their complete lack of social skills gave Eve an almost immediate, kin–like bond with the basement dwellers.

As she and SAC Lange dropped down the five levels to the space where the magic happened, Eve thought she knew what to expect: young disheveled-looking men, not necessarily very hygienic, as if they spent their time off doing just the same thing they did at work, but alone. She imagined the office space to be humming with cooling fans over electronic circuits, computers in all states of use and disuse, some with their guts spilling out and parts hijacked to repair others, and an overall aroma of unwashed bodies, leftovers, and soda bottles everywhere.

Eve remembered touring the Operational Technology Division at Quantico, with their team of agents, engineers, electronic technologists, forensic examiners, and analysts. She never anticipated that the same level of well-appointed, dedicated space could be found underground at the NYC field office. What she walked into was a far cry from her expectations. A space nearly as big as a football field was sliced up for various, well-defined uses. SAC Lange ushered her to a conference room where sat an array of professionals that varied in age, look, and gender. The only common theme in the room was the universal look of intelligence. SAC Lange shook hands with a man who sported a politician's head of gray hair, a warm smile, and impeccable dress. Lange looked at Eve, then back at the gentleman, and said "Good luck."

The first thing out of Eve's mouth was "Wow, I had no idea."

The gray-haired gentlemen introduced himself, "Greetings Eve, I am Mr. Smith." Eve covered her laugh with a cough, "Could he sound any more clandestine?" Mr. Smith went on to introduce Eve to the rest of the assembled team. Franklin, Harry, Joan, and Wenjun.

Franklin stood up and walked over to Eve, standing so

close she had to resist the urge to back up. His accent was elegant, very upper-class British sounding. He reminded her of Alistair. She learned later that he was the son of an American diplomat. Harry and Joan stood up together, almost knocking each other over. Their laughter was genuine, and Eve could tell that, unbeknownst to them, they were crushing on each other. She would have to fix that. Wenjun was slow to stand and after a careful adjustment of her glasses, she nodded to Eve, and then immediately sat back down. This was her dream team, those tasked to complete her transformation.

Eve did not try to hide her surprise, "Wow, I didnt know this place existed," with a quick glance around the room, "And that your budget was so ummm... generous."

Franklin, speaking as one with a powerful personality and a healthy ego to match, responded, "If computers were suddenly unable to work, the world would fall apart, planes would be grounded, cars would stall in the middle of the roads, phones, and other communication devices would be wasted bits of plastic." The other FBI team members nodded their heads in agreement. Eve sensed the narrative was repeated often to dispel any doubts about the value of the FBI's computer masters.

Eve would soon find out that each of the team members had a specialty that made them vital to her transformation. Franklin's purpose on the team was to address the overall digital transition of Eve to Dr. Nicole Mathers. Harry was responsible for Dr. Mather's publications. The first step he explained, was to hire a couple ghostwriters to quickly pull together a couple of non-fiction books that would solidify her place as a terrorism researcher. The next step was to reach out to a few pay-to-publish vanity presses and give them a few extra dollars to get articles placed in past journal editions, establishing a publication history.

Joan's responsibility was to give Nicole a history, not simply as a researcher or author, but a past that could stand up to high-level digging. Wenjun would be Nicole's social media guru: Blogs, podcasts, Facebook, Instagram, whatever it took to turn Dr. Nicole Mathers into an overnight star.

Unfortunately for Eve, this would be a lot of work on her part as well. This imaginary persona would have to be so ingrained that she should have difficulty distinguishing the fantasy from her own reality.

When the mission, known simply as The Academic, had first crossed his desk, Harry had immediately called Professor Malcolm at UCLA, an old college fraternity brother from his time at Berkley. Eve was fascinated to learn that the FBI hired English majors, that there existed professionals who were called upon for missions such as this.

One such person was Professor Khalid, currently holding a tenured position at UCLA. He received the call between a faculty meeting and class. They wanted him to ghostwrite a book with a Berkeley sociology professor who had expertise in terrorism, specifically American terrorism. Berkeley would send the synopsis and references, and Khalid would turn it into a book. The part that concerned him the most was that upon receipt of the rough manuscript, he would only have a turnaround time of thirty days. That would be 3,000 words a day. It was time to set up a meeting with his grad students to take over his classes and to tell the chair he needed a brief sabbatical.

Harry had an artificial intelligence computer program that could write academic style papers with very little supervision. He simply typed in a variety of related key words. The computer looked in databases using the key words in different groupings, quickly identified the top researchers in the field, their most cited papers, and gaps in the literature. It then generated an outline based on the keywords, scanned the journal articles, and created a unique academic review article in a matter of minutes.

The next thing Harry had to do was to contact pay-to-publish journals and offer them incentive to put the journal articles in back dated papers. This would demonstrate that Dr. Mathers had a long history of publishing in the field of terrorism. He managed to convince twenty journals to publish the articles over a span of fifteen years, to include time as a doctoral student and a post doc position.

The book that Berkley and UCLA created was a non-fiction book, *The Mindset of a Terrorist*. It was exactly what Harry wanted, and they finished on time, as he knew they would.

The AI computer was able to generate the second book, *The American Terrorist: Everything You Need to Know to be a Subject Matter Expert*. The computer collected data on American citizens charged with terrorism, identifying several different variables of interest and looked for patterns in the data. It came back with thirty-eight figures, nine tables, and paragraphs of unplagiarized facts that supported the figures and tables.

This was the first time that Henry had used the AI to create an entire book and he was very impressed with the outcome.

As he skimmed through the text, Harry thought it should be easy enough for Eve to read and understand. He was not 100% confident she was going to succeed, however. Eve seemed almost unreachable, perhaps even on the Autism spectrum. He would have to quiz her thoroughly before she headed to the conference. In fact, it would be a good idea to create some cliff notes, with pictures, just in case. Harry sat down at his desk and sent a text to Eve to meet with him the following day.

The FBI has a few connections at some of the top publishing houses in the world and, within minutes of completion, the books had ISBN numbers and were available on Amazon and other online bookstores. Two copies of each went to the Library of Congress and two copies were sent upstairs to SAC Lange and Special Agent Black.

Joan carried her iPad with her everywhere she went, even into the ladies' room. She was intensely worried that someone would clone it, or damage it in some way. Her paranoia was over the top, and likely unnecessary, but that's who she was and there was no changing her.

Joan liked Eve as soon as she met her. She felt a connection, kindred spirits, unheard of between a special agent and a computer geek. She wanted to impress Eve with her skills and give her the best background the FBI could afford. Joan listened to Eve speak and decided she could pass as someone born in

Oregon. Before lunch, she had put together a package for Eve that included hometown, schools and teachers, best friends, and popular hangouts. She even Photoshopped a young-looking Eve into school uniforms and swapped the images with a student who resembled Eve. Little Nicole Mathers, from small-town Oregon, who would grow up, (in contrast to the real Nicole Mathers, a missionary in Haiti) to become a well-respected terrorism researcher.

Joan had a couple interns that helped her get fake application records, transcripts, and graduation diplomas into her high school and colleges, and made sure Eve had won a few awards along the way. In fact, she had recently been awarded a grant by the DOJ. That was an easy one to pull off. The grant was a team effort including Dr. Mathers, computer scientist, and a psychologist, to scan social media sites for radical hate talk.

As fake Eve/Nicole aged, the altered images reflected it. Graduations, parties, family photos, Joan created them and sent them over to Wenjun, known affectionately by the group as Wennie. The last thing Joan had to do was to create a Curriculum Vitae for Nicole and paste it on various sites on the internet. When Joan and the FBI interns were done, they hired an investigator to find out everything they could on Dr. Nicole Mathers and to give them a summation of her life. The results were as predicted, and they packed up the material and sent it to Eve to study.

Eve had the opportunity to sit down with Wennie and watch her do her thing. Wennie may have been a shy Japanese girl but get her on social media and she was a superstar. She created a Facebook account and then gave it a soft delete. A soft delete is when a member deletes his or her account, but with the right software the account can still be discovered. Wennie also found a Twitter account that belonged to someone near Eve's age that had died, and with a few clicks turned that ten-year account into Nicole's Twitter. The photos Joan had sent over were already embedded in the accounts and in other locations, tagged by imaginary friends, and it felt so real Eve could almost believe it herself. Eve complimented Wennie on her skills and thanked her for her hard work. Wennie blushed and thanked Eve for her compliments.

Eve's curiosity was piqued, and she asked Wennie what she wanted to be doing in five or ten years. Wennie looked at her and said earnestly, "Exactly what I am doing here. This is my dream job."

Eve laughed, "Well then, dear Wennie, I am glad that you are part of my dream team."

Eve was sent home with stacks of papers, two books, her CV, passwords, and her own tablet with electronic versions of everything in her bag now. It would take several days to study and learn everything. Time was short. She looked at the calendar. The IDEC was only a week away.

When Eve met with Harry the next day, he briefed her on the books and publications, and impressed upon her the fact that she would have to memorize and understand all of it. Harry was not a nice man, nor was he very friendly, but Eve respected his professionalism. "May explain why he and Joan have never confessed their feelings," she mused.

"Harry, have you and Joan worked together for very long?" His expression immediately changed. He had a hard, all-business face, but there was a slight dilation of the pupils, a momentary pause before he answered. She was sure she was correct; he did have feelings for Joan that went beyond their work.

"This is the first mission we worked on together, but we've been at this location for five years."

"Have the two of you been dating long?"

"What are you talking about," he sputtered, "We're not dating."

"Oh, that is a shame, she clearly likes you. When we were together you were the only thing she talked about," she lied.

"Really?" Harry's face lit up.

Oh man, he had it bad. "I would suggest that, if you haven't asked her out, you do so very soon. She may not wait forever."

"I will, thank you, Eve." And he thought to himself, "Maybe she does have what it takes to succeed in this mission," although he was still worried her emotions would get the best of her and she would forget her place. As long as she could work her way out of a disagreement without pulling her gun, or punching someone, then it should be a successful mission. Harry had done his homework on Eve, researched her previous missions, style, and successes. He knew she could be a hot mess, but that mattered very little as long as she did not interfere with the mission's success. Eve as Dr. Mathers was merely the tool to make it happen. He hoped they had chosen well.

That evening Eve packed for her trip to Ohio. Her Burberry luggage was beautiful. She placed her new clothes in them with care. All her life she had been poor. Sure, she had food and people that cared about her, but for birthdays and Christmas she had received gifts of books and telescopes and field guides. No one in SFH considered clothes and beauty important. In fact, they scoffed at people who prioritized such things. Eve held up one of the Haute Couture dresses and smiled critically. "This cost more than most people make in a month," she mused. She carefully lay the dress on the bed and picked up the $700 Louboutin's. She had to acknowledge they were beautiful, but they were more expensive than any shoes had the right to be. On top of that, they were the most uncomfortable shoes she had ever worn. There should be a law: elite cost equals elite comfort. If one can pay for such expensive things, one should at least be comfortable.

After packing her bags, she changed into a big t-shirt and sat on her bed surrounded by everything that made her Dr. Nicole Mathers. She poured herself a glass of wine, skimmed over the books and read the abstracts on the journal articles. The articles in their entirety were too much to absorb so late at night.

She slept through the night. When she woke, she felt a sense of excitement. This was to be her first big undercover assignment and she was pretty sure she could handle it. Seriously, how hard could it be to fool a bunch of men that preferred guns over books? Eve stood in front of her mirror. It was not a full-length mirror. She had never felt the need to see herself from head to toe, but today she wished she could. The image that was reflected back was one that boosted her confidence. She felt emboldened by this put-together woman looking back at her, no need to hide in the shadows, nor to avoid human contact. She could face whatever was thrust at her. Maybe there was something to this whole style thing.

Okay, maybe she was kidding herself. She really didn't believe she could ever prefer a crowd of people to a night home alone with a book. She had worked too hard to keep people at a distance and no amount of fancy clothes would change that about her.

Chapter Seven

IDEC Opening Ceremony

By the time the plane landed, Eve was already in the game. She was unsure how her SAC was able to fund a first-class ticket. Around the office the line, "It's well known that the DHS has all the money," was the comeback whenever anyone in the office asked for a new computer, an ergonomic chair, or a bigger budget to pay informants. She decided that if she could get used to the clothes, she could get used to first class. During the flight, Eve determined to brush up on her flirting by doing so with the flight attendants, male and female. She did not discriminate. When she disembarked, she had more than one of them hand her their phone numbers. As soon she was out of their view, Eve crumbled up the scraps of paper and tossed them into the closest trash receptacle. She almost fell. Damn heels.

The only thing that saved her from ending up on the ground with her dress up around her waist was the gentleman walking next to her. He gracefully held her in his arms for a moment, and then made sure she was safely on her feet before releasing her. He gave her a pleasant smile. She thanked him and asked him what brought him to Cincinnati. He joked that, aside from catching damsels as they fell, he was returning from a conference. He was a professor of art at the University of Cincinnati. She glanced at his hand, and an unmarried one too. He handed her his card. This one she kept.

A sign with Dr. Mathers name was in the hands of a very attractive man. She knew him to be Agent Coppo, one of the guys from the Cincinnati field office. He was to be her chauffeur for the trip. He was there to make sure she had immediate backup and support. He carried her bags to the car and transported her to the hotel without breaking cover. She thought to herself that she could learn a lot from this man.

The Cincinnatian Hotel was chosen for her because of its 4-star luxury and elegant atmosphere. If Eve was going to come across as a top-selling author, she had to live the part. She was impressed with the attention to detail her team managed to pull off in such a short time frame. As she walked through the hotel lobby, she was fascinated with the look of this boutique hotel, its high ceilings, contemporary furnishings, large windows, and the beautiful artwork. It felt both comfortable and clean, like a place where she could unwind. Eve looked around the lobby and spotted Sergei Bodrovi, the well-known Surface-to-Air missile representative. He looked just as she remembered, dark hair and even darker eyes. His black suit covered a muscular body that emphasized his strength and power within the arms community.

Her dream team had managed to hack the conference webpage and obtain a list of attendees and vendors. After studying his bio, she felt like she already knew him, and the way he stared at her, it was clear he wanted to get to know her. She gave him a smile and thought, "Here we go."

"Sergei, it is sooo wonderful to see you again," she gushed, "It has been a few years, since the conference in Barcelona."

Sergei had no idea who this lovely creature was, but he was not about to admit it. "Ah, yes, and you are looking as beautiful as the first time I set eyes on you."

Before he could ask, Eve elaborated on her identity. "I have published another book since we last met, perhaps you have read it, *The American Terrorist?*"

He professed with regret that he had not yet read it but would get a copy right away and perhaps they could meet later for an autograph? Eve said that would be lovely, if her schedule allowed, gave him two light kisses, one on each cheek, and then proceeded to give him a hug that involved so much sensuality she felt the need for an immediate shower.

When she departed, Bodrovi dropped his smile and turned to an assistant and said, "Find out everything you can on that woman and have it to me by dinner." He knew there was something unique about her, but he could not put his finger on it.

When Eve walked up to the reception desk, she caught Vic lounging in one of the leather chairs, reading a *CBRNe World* magazine. She glanced down at the *Vogue* peeking out of her red Hermes Birkin handbag and thought to herself that life can be unfair and going undercover sucks.

When Vic saw her walking over, he stood and gave her a slight bow. Eve was impressed with his transformation. He was wearing a Bespoke Brioni Tonal Stripe Wool suit, and if her memory of shopping at Sacs served her correctly, the cost was easily seven figures. His shoes were beautiful Berluti Scritto brown leather. One thing for sure, Vic had money and was an immaculate dresser. This had not come through at their first meeting and Eve pondered the idea that the Vic she met in the interrogation room may have been a well-played act. Of course, her own transformation process had given her new insights. The man in front of her resembled that man in name and general appearance only. Even his manner of speaking had changed, from Jersey slang to an educated, ivy league mid-Atlantic accent.

Vic offered his arm and escorted Eve to the lounge, while the bellhops carefully arranged her luggage onto the cart and took it up to her room. The offered arm was dual purpose. It was a gentlemanly way to escort a woman, but it also aided in keeping Eve on her feet. She had been wearing the heels all day and was feeling a bit wobbly.

"When this mission is over," Eve told herself, "I will never wear a heeled shoe again in my life." She was more certain than ever that they were a torture device created by men to keep women down, to perpetuate the belief that woman were mere adornments with little value and less sense. Thoughts like this were starting to anger Eve and she pulled her arm away from Vic in such a way that it startled both him and a few hotel guests nearby.

Eve ordered a dirty martini and Vic had a Cardinale. The two walked around the lounge reacquainting themselves (or in Eve's case, acquainting) with other conference attendees. After their cocktails, Eve excused herself to freshen up for the evening's opening ceremony festivities.

When she got up to her room, Eve was surprised to see her luggage had been emptied, her belongings had been put away neatly, and a red binder was lying on the bed. She picked it up and remembered where she had last seen it. Samantha had generously put this together for her. It listed the attire, hairstyle, makeup, and jewelry she should be wearing for all expected encounters, and, to Eve's surprise and chagrin, it included photos of her in the dressing rooms from their day of shopping together. She scanned the pages of the binder, determined to wear these outfits with confidence. She knew that the FBI had strategically placed undercover agents throughout the locations where she would be spending time during the mission. This must have included hotel bell boys.

Eve met Vic in the lobby and together they took Eve's private car to the Convention Center. It was barely a five-minute drive, but, when parking and bad weather and high heels are accounted for, a private car was always to be preferred. Eve was not sure she could walk a half a mile in her current jeweled Manolo Blahniks, a.k.a. someone paid too much for another pair of uncomfortable shoes. Eve chided herself. Not the kind of person to grumble, she found herself indulging in a constant internal monologue of complaints with every change of wardrobe. She promised herself this was the last time. She would rise to the occasion. Other women dressed this way every day. She could too.

The convention center looked like every other one Eve had been in, but when they arrived in the room where the opening celebrations were being held, the room had an opulent, over-the-top feel. Arms dealing was clearly lucrative and one look around the room convinced Eve that the people in the field had no problems displaying their wealth on their person, as well as on the lavish decorations surrounding them.

Servers circulated around the room with platters of hors d'oeuvres and glasses of wine and champagne. Eve's alcohol tolerance was low. After witnessing her father's downward spiral upon her mother's departure, and the bar patrons in college, she tended to avoid the stuff. She hated to be at a disadvantage, but she accepted a glass of champagne and plastered a smile on her face. To all that observed her, she looked to be having a wonderful time, mingling and drinking. In fact, Eve was having a good time, reading the room, sizing up all the attendees.

One trend she noticed was the large number of couples. To be specific, not-so-attractive middle-aged men, paired with tall, perfectly tanned, model types. It was clear to Eve that many of the women were simply arm candy and extensions of the men's wealth. Eve was definitely not the model type. She was far too curvy to resemble these runway girls. Eve liked to eat. She enjoyed desserts. The only thing that allowed her to pass the FBI's demanding physical exams was her time at the gym. This evening she wore a beautiful off-the-shoulder velvet sheath dress that flattered her curves, matching very well with her emerald green eyes. Her hair was styled in a chignon that accentuated her long neck and pale skin. Eve felt grateful to have the genes of a black-Irish father and a Scandinavian mother.

When Eve found the opportunity, she walked up to the Lebanese-born, Ukrainian arms dealer and Hezbollah operative, Mr. Ali Amin. She asked him if he was still with Ukrspecexport. He seemed impressed that she knew this about him and told her that not only was he promoted to vice president, but he was also serving as an advisor to former Ukrainian President Viktor Yanukovych. She congratulated him on his promotion. Mr. Amin dealt in surface to air missiles. Eve was not sure if she would ever need any missiles, but the connection could be valuable. She handed him her card and said it was nice seeing him again and asked him to send his brother her love as well. His brother was a well-known, handsome playboy and Hezbollah leader.

It should not have surprised her as much as it did to see international arms trafficker, Ukraine born, Mr. Leonid Minin. The last thing she heard was that Italian authorities arrested him near Milan. Minin's talents went beyond arms dealing. He was considered quite good at falsifying identity documents and he was a well-known art thief.

She approached him with an outstretched arm to introduce herself when she was pulled into a bear hug. His hands traveled up and down her back and her breasts were crushed against him.

"Ah, Dr. Mathers, I am so excited (and yes, unfortunately, she could tell he was very excited) to meet you. I heard about your latest book and was hoping you would do a private book signing."

"I've got this," she said to herself, "I am not going to hurt him, I am not going to hurt him..." a mantra she was sure she would be repeating several times before the conference was over. "Mr. Minin, how lovely to meet you, your reputation precedes you as well."

"Please call me Leo." He kissed her on each cheek. Eve closed her fists tightly and kept them at her sides.

"Leo, I do not have a book signing planned, but let's meet during the conference and chat, I would be happy to sign your book."

He confessed, he did not have her book, but would be delighted to buy one and catch her later. Leo was pleased he had seen her poster earlier in the day and had thought to himself she was one fine looking lady. Oh yes, he wanted her.

Several of the people she had met earlier in the lounge were here this evening and greeted Eve and Vic like old friends. Eve noticed when she talked about her latest book that the crowd near her increased in size considerably. Eve managed to field many of the questions with ease. She was very proud of herself; she had done her homework. It wasn't hard, she had found the book quite interesting.

At one point, a man approached her and in a not quite friendly manner introduced himself as Joseph Carvallo. He wanted to know more about her academic appointment. The amount of studying Eve had to do about the department, the school, and university, even the surrounding city, was extensive and tedious, and she wasn't 100% sure she remembered all of the minutiae correctly. The way he looked at her, his eyes drilling into her soul, made her question herself even more. When he walked away, she pulled out her phone and texted her dream team.

Within minutes she received an encrypted text, Joseph Nicholas Carvallo, born in NYC, joined the Army Military Police. After serving six years, he was dishonorably discharged for a weapons violation. Carvallo went on to get his bachelor's degree in international studies and an MBA degree. He was believed to be a major exporter of military grade weapons and considered very dangerous.

Throughout the evening, every time she looked in his direction, she was met with staring eyes that pierced her like an arrow. Carvallo did not try to hide the fact that he was watching her. Vic picked up on the behavior and offered to go start up a conversation. Eve could not see the harm and wished him luck. She could tell from his body language that this Carvallo person was going to be trouble for her; it was just a matter of time. If Vic could uncover some information about the man, all the better.

When Eve met the ravishing, dark-eyed beauty, Nadia Leah Katz, they were both observing a 3D weapons training simulation in the vender's center. The men behind the booth thought it would be fun to invite the two women to try the training simulation together. They looked at each other and agreed. As they suited up, the gear over their cocktail dresses sparked the interest of several of the men in the room, who promptly gathered to watch them on the viewing screen.

The simulation started out in a crowded urban setting. The graphics were amazing: the sidewalks had mud puddles, cracks in the pavement, and a barking dog leashed to a stop sign. There was even a little boy in a red raincoat and yellow galoshes playing near a couple of ladies looking like they worked the streets. Not far from sim-Eve was a drug deal going down. At the moment the two dealers caught her eye, her opponent phased in, raised a Jericho 941 handgun, and started shooting. Eve took cover behind a car that was missing its tires, and flipped through her online arsenal, which gave her opponent time to reload. The sim-fighting continued for a few more minutes, each of the woman getting in several good hits.

Eve knew she should let her opponent win, there is no way an academic like Dr. Nicole Mathers would be so good, but she could not help herself. With such a crowd and against a woman, her competitive nature won out, and the two were head-to-head until the very end. That's when it happened: she let her guard down and got knifed in her simulated neck... game over. So much blood squirted from the fake wound that Eve felt slightly queasy. The audience applauded and when their gear was removed someone from the gathered crowd asked them what they did. Her opponent, Nadia, replied that she was a weapons trainer for the Israeli army. Eve knew she had messed up. A researcher or author would not have lasted a minute with a trained professional and they had been going at it for 10 minutes. They waited for her response and so, thinking quickly on her feet she said, "if I tell you...,"

And everyone replied in unison "I'd have to kill you." Several in the audience laughed and then dispersed.

Nadia said to Eve that she owed the champion a drink, tucked her arm under Eve's, and walked to one of the drink islands spread throughout the venue. "You know the drinks are free, right?" Eve quipped.

"Oh yes, but it's the thought that counts, besides I want to know more about you," Nadia leaned into her conspiratorially.

Eve knew better than to have another drink. She was already feeling light-headed and quite possibly tipsy. After that simulation, her adrenaline was high, and she wouldn't mind getting to know Nadia better too.

With drinks in their hands, the two went off to enjoy their beverages and to talk. As the evening wore on, the other conference attendees consumed more alcohol and got stupid. The two pretty ladies were more temptation than they could handle and drunken men, used to getting what they wanted, approached them one after another. Finally, the women had enough of rebuffing the unwanted attention and stepped outside to get a break. After several minutes of small talk, Nadia finally said to Eve, "Okay, your pivot when asked about your work did not go unnoticed, what do you do?"

Eve didn't know how to answer. She did not want to lie to Nadia, but she was not prepared to blow her cover either. The best she could come up with in the moment was, "I can't tell you."

Nadia said, "Perhaps someday you will tell me," and let the conversation drop. Eve did not ask Nadia about her work. She was never any good at small talk, especially when it came to asking people about things that didn't matter to her. When Eve said she had to go, Nadia asked for her phone number. Eve hesitantly gave it to her. Nadia asked for Eve's cell, typed what looked like gibberish, and handed the phone back to Eve. "My number."

When Eve stood up to leave, she noticed her car and driver were right in front of her. She figured Vic could find his own way home and got into the car. Her room looked just as she had left it. She slipped off her shoes and flung herself onto her bed. One or two stretches later, she lay there, enjoying the peace and quiet, wriggling her toes and for a short time, she felt pure bliss.

Then the phone chimed. It was Vic.

"Did you learn anything from Carvallo?" She asked.

"Well, first off, thanks for leaving me, and no, he was very tight-lipped." Eve told Vic she knew he could take care of himself and he chortled, "And on that note, I have work to do, still arranging your interviews, so I will see you tomorrow. By the way, Leonid Minin was throwing your name around earlier, I think he believes the two of you will be having an assignation during this conference."

Eve laughed, "Not a chance," and hung up the phone.

The next call came less than five minutes from the last and Eve picked up the phone, "What now?" It was her dream-team leader, Franklin.

"Eve, we've been monitoring the internet, specifically IPs around your location and there has been a lot of chatter, people googling Dr. Nicole Mathers. Do we have any reason to be concerned?"

Eve thought about the possible outcomes if she mentioned her gaffe with the simulation game or the misgivings, she had regarding Mr. Joseph Carvallo and his unusual interest in her. If she told Franklin the truth, she was pretty sure she would be yanked from the mission. She could not let that happen. She was not fooling herself. She wasn't very good at this undercover work, but she didn't want to give up. She had her own personal reasons.

If Franklin already knew something was up, she could be caught in a lie. It was a tough decision. "Well, Franklin, I must say my encounters with Mr. Carvallo have left me feeling a little uncomfortable. I was just debating whether I should personally do something about it, or let your team come up with some suggestions. I was leaning more to you guys working on it and getting back with me tomorrow, what do you think?"

Eve believed that flattery and giving him the power to decide would stop him from taking the chatter issue any further, and she was correct. He found the idea a good one and assured Eve they would get back with her tomorrow. "But in the meantime, remember, you are Dr. Nicole Mathers, don't fuck that up!" Wow, it was almost as if he knew.

"Really, Franklin, you do not have a single nice thing to say to me?" Eve asked in a very flirty way.

There was a noted silence before Franklin responded. "Beautiful and deadly Eve, is there really anything I need to say that you don't already know?"

Eve smiled to herself and said, "Why Franklin that may be the nicest thing anyone has ever said to me."

"Goodnight Eve." She hung up the phone without replying.

Just one more thing before slipping into the shower. Eve looked up Nadia's number and texted her a simple goodnight. She needed an ally in case trouble broke out, and she could not imagine any better than an Israeli weapons trainer. Sure, she had Vic, but she was certain he would flip if he thought that doing so would keep him out of prison or save his life.

After a hot shower, she wrapped up in the plush hotel robe and picked up her files on the first three interviews. They were all domestic hate groups. The first one, Campbell, was some environmental nut job that probably hadn't bathed in weeks. Then she was scheduled to meet the leader of the Hutaree militia group. She was sure Joshua would have a low IQ and wear nothing but camouflage. The last meeting was with a couple of Aryan Nation members. She had met a few of them in the past. Their philosophies were vile, and she wondered how they ended up hating so many people simply because they were different. What cards were they dealt that made them blame others for their own shortcomings? It was her psychology degree rearing its academic head. Maybe someday she would infiltrate the group and learn more.

As she lay there in bed reflecting on her day, Franklin kept popping into her head, his accent, his arrogance. She knew she had a thing for British men, she supposed even faux British, like him. They were both aphrodisiacs to Eve, but she was not about to get into a relationship. The last one had not turned out so well.

His name was Aaron Racher. He had been at Quantico training to be an analyst. It was right after the training program was restructured to have the first half of agent training done concurrently with the analysts, so they learned how to work together as a team. Eve had taken a liking to him right away, his big blue eyes, dark hair. And there was his magnificent, athletic body. It had set him apart from the majority of analysts working hard just to pass the physical exams.

Hogan's Alley was a realistic urban setting training ground for trainees. During their training, Eve and Aaron ended up taking down some heavily armed drug smugglers in a townhouse where four hostages were being held. That night, celebrating their success, they had done a little too much celebrating and ended up in bed together. She had awakened to scents of hot, greasy sausages frying in the skillet and powdery-sweet waffles. She had inhaled deeply and realized this was the first time she had been with someone without having a clear plan, an endgame. Aaron seemed to be really into her as well.

Their relationship had continued to grow, but as the time had drawn near for Aaron to go on his first assignment, he had become more and more restless and bad-tempered. Then, the night before his departure, they had gone hiking. It was still early in the evening when they emerged onto a beach near the Potomac. She had believed it was purely accidental until she noticed the blanket lying on the sand, complete with picnic basket and wine chiller.

"Oh, bloody hell." She knew what was coming. The mischievous smile he had worn on his face all day, the unusual pep in his step. "Oh, holy mother, he's going to fucking propose." Nothing could have soured her mood more than the cliché that lay before her. Aaron witnessed it. The obvious dismay and near revulsion that appeared on Eve's face said it all. He had let loose, telling Eve how she was a broken sociopath that only cared about herself and should die alone and did not deserve him. She had tried to console him and had reached for him, but he wasn't having it and had shrugged her away, "Get away from me you cold bitch, you will regret this!" He had grabbed the bottle of wine, uncorked it and took off down the river.

Eve had simply stood there for a moment, dumb-struck. It was such a beautiful day. A warm breeze gently cooled her after the rigorous hike. She sat on the blanket, opened the basket and, to her delight, saw a delicious looking ham and cheese sandwich.

She unwrapped it, closed her eyes, and enjoyed the meal.

Eve awoke to her alarm going off and she jumped out of the hotel bed, a little too quickly because her head was pounding. She went into the bathroom, took care of business, popped a few pain pills, threw on some sweats and shoes, and went down to the hotel gym. Working out invigorated her. She found it to be a great way to start her day.

Chapter Eight

Conference Day One

Eve was armed, not with her Glock .40 caliber, but with her notebook, predefined questions, and a smile. In character as Dr. Nicole Mathers, she was sitting in a private conference room at the convention center. It was a comfortable space, mahogany wood giving off the scents of lemon and old books, with beverages and breakfast goods on the credenza, live plants, and artwork depicting beautiful landscapes from around the world.

The first prearranged meeting was with Campbell

Greene, an informal leader of the ELF organization. The Earth Liberation Front (ELF), an eco-terror group, had worked with its sister group, the Animal Liberation Front (ALF), to do almost 50 million dollars in damage to farmers, scientists, foresters, universities, housing developers and business owners.

Campbell had been wanted by the FBI as a domestic terrorist for several years, and the fact that she would be meeting him today excited her. Eve had received his dossier well in advance and her outfit was chosen to appeal to his sensibilities. She wore her auburn hair long and natural, very little makeup, but still carefully applied, with a simple wrap dress that reminded one of spring gardens, and a pair of modest flats.

Campbell walked in and took a seat without acknowledging Eve. It gave her a moment to size him up. This vegan anarchist was just as she imagined, the only thing missing was a wheat grass smoothie, a marijuana cigarette, and some 1970s music. At that moment she realized the person she had in mind was a young version of her father, and the man that entered the room supported that vision. He sported a trendy hairstyle, a vigorous, messy textured top, undercut fade, complete with full beard. His jeans were faded, but clean, and his unassuming t-shirt had the words "STOP KILLING OUR PLANET" sprawled across the front. Like his jeans, the words were faded, but the meaning was not.

Eve started the conversation telling Campbell how much she appreciated his shirt and gave him a brief description of her own life living with nature at the commune. She shared that those experiences allowed her to appreciate people that will do what it takes to protect the planet. Eve never even noticed that she was providing this domestic terrorist with her own personal history, not that of Dr. Mathers.

He finally met Eve's eyes and smiled at her. He admitted, "There's a line a lot of people are not willing to cross. I am willing." After a little bit of prodding on Eve's part, he went on to say that he had grown up in Seattle, Washington, before Starbucks arrived, which in his humble opinion single-handedly ruined the city. Eve was immediately thankful she had downed about a gallon of black coffee in her hotel room this morning and was now nursing an organic green tea instead of a Starbucks coffee. She offered a cup of tea to Campbell, who took it, approvingly.

Eve had a set list of questions she was instructed to ask Campbell, but she strayed from the list with a few questions of her own. She first asked why he got involved. Campbell said his first involvement with ELF was at the second major mobilization of the antiglobalization movement, known as N30, which he said occurred late in 1999.

His face shone and he sat up and leaned forward in his seat. He went on to tell Eve about the protesters blocking the delegates' entrance to the World Trade Organization meetings in Seattle. The protests forced the cancellation of the opening ceremonies and lasted four days. Police had fired tear gas at the demonstrators. Over 600 protesters, Campbell included, were arrested. Thousands were injured. Three policemen were injured by friendly fire, and one by a rock, thrown by a protestor. Some protesters had targeted businesses, such as a large Nike shop and his despised Starbucks. They had broken windows, spray-painted buildings, and vandalized merchandise, exposed by the broken windows. He said that this was when they had realized that the use of violence garners attention. He also realized he was committed to the cause, come what may.

Eve next asked about leadership and how they kept themselves protected from the law. He shared that ELF was made up of small cells all over the world and that they were unaware of one another's identities and plans. Campbell leaned in and whispered, apparently afraid someone was listening, "We took the initiative and created our own cell, we take care of each other, live off the grid, and have no need for the government's involvement."

At this Eve had to grin, but it was from the heart and caused a sparkle in her eyes. "Campbell, you sound so much like my father when he was a young man, I wish you could meet him." She allowed her hand to rest lightly on his, but only briefly. His eyes looked into hers and she stared back just long enough to send a message, then dropped her gaze and asked the next question.

Eve wanted to know how they pick their targets. She knew that when the group got their start in December 1999, they firebombed targets that did not appear to be relevant to their cause. ELF burned the plant genetics laboratories at Michigan State University and the University of Washington. They started fires at a Nike outlet in Albertville, Minn., and even targeted the Republican Party Committee headquarters.

Campbell did not openly admit to his involvement

in those acts but laughed when she mentioned the Republican Party Committee HQ.

"They supported the extension of an interstate highway, one that would decrease the greenspace in Indiana."

She realized that ELF's targets were intended to leave people wondering why and to make it difficult to predict future targets.

Eve thanked Campbell for his honesty and said she hoped they could meet again, to which he proposed dinner at a great vegan place nearby. Eve said she would be delighted to have dinner and rose, as a signal that the meeting was over. She gave him her business card and, on his way, out the door, he looked back and said. "One more thing: I'm not advocating for the slaughter of innocents, but humans are destroying the planet and there's a need for decreasing the population."

Eve breathed a sigh of relief when the door shut. She was quickly losing any enthusiasm she had for undercover work. She found the encounter with Campbell Greene exhausting. She wished that the dinner was not necessary. There was nothing more she would rather do than have room service back at the hotel and binge on Netflix. Eve had to rush back to the hotel to change for the next interview. She knew this was going to be interesting.

The meeting was with the leader of the Hutaree organization from Michigan. Her experience with militia groups was limited. The FBI kept a close eye on them, the Hutaree in particular. In fact, she remembered one of her Quantico friends going undercover with them for a year or so and sharing some fascinating stories, one involving a wedding with a camouflage theme.

Eve laughed inwardly when she read that they though they called themselves Christian warriors, they plotted to kill a policeman and bomb his funeral. More like warrior wannabes, flying under the flag of Christianity to give them an air of legitimacy, and not appear as the backward, inbred group they were. Camilla had been deeply religious and a devout Catholic. Neither her father nor Eve felt the calling, though they were often comforted by Camilla's prayers, candles, and rosary. To take the name of something that means so much to the world and use it to sanction killing infuriated Eve. Yes, she knew her history. She knew her anger made little sense, but she felt it, never-the-less.

When she got back to her hotel, she pulled out her notebook and looked at the attire for the Hutaree meeting: gold cross necklace, light pink nail polish, hair straightened and then slight waves applied, subtle makeup, and small diamond post earrings. She was to wear a long maxi flowing classic light gray skirt, with a woven polyester white blouse. The blouse had a front bow, long sleeves with button cuffs, and a slightly curved hem. One look in the mirror and Eve knew she could convey the demeanor of an innocent submissive. It was not just her outward appearance and posture that had to change; her vocabulary had to be altered as well.

When she first arrived back at the conference room, she had to step back outside the room and look at the number above the door, 012, to be certain it was the same room. She went back in and looked around. The works of art had been removed and in their place were images with biblical themes. She read the plaques that accompanied each piece, *The Garden of Earthly Delights* by Hieronymus Bosch, Caravaggio's *David and Goliath*, *The Annunciation* by El Greco, and *The Building of the Ark* by Bertram of Minden. The beverages and snacks were simple, and Eve even noticed the Bible now on the bookshelf in front of the wall opposite the door. She had a few minutes before the Hutaree leader, Mr. Joshua Carter, would arrive. She slipped off her shoes so she could enjoy the soft carpet for just a few minutes. Weeks of practicing in heels had left her feet in a constant state of pain.

It wasn't long before Mr. Carter knocked on the door and Eve opened it. There stood a man that reminded her of the evil Reverend Kane from the Poltergeist movies, a bit more weight on him, but the same creepy vibe. She moved out of the way so he could walk past her into the room. Not out of deference as he probably assumed, she was just worried their bodies would touch. She followed him in, and because he was ahead of her, he got to choose his seat. Then, with a tilt of his head and an expansive sweep of his arm, he gestured for her to take a seat. "What an ostentatious ass," she thought. At least Campbell was enjoyable. This guy was going to push all her buttons.

It was time for her to show deference and submissiveness, which were the most difficult characteristics for her to perform convincingly. Once seated, she rounded her shoulders, dropped her head ever so slightly and looked up at him. This was only possible because of her hunched posture. "Good afternoon Mr. Carter. My name is Dr. Mathers. I want to thank you for taking the time today to speak to me about your militia group and giving me the opportunity to share your side of the story. It is quite a privilege for me to sit and talk with you. I don't know if you are aware that my upbringing was very similar." My father chose to lead a group of us out to the desert in New Mexico so we could live a life far from the reaches of the government and nonbelievers." While not entirely accurate it was enough to sound believable, she thought.

He patted her on the hand and said, "Sure thing, honey, we church-going folks have to stick together."

Eve still did not notice that she was once again sharing her own past, not that of Dr. Mathers. "Sir, my first questions are straight forward. What made you form this group and what is your endgame?"

"Well, honey our endgame is heaven. When Christ comes to get us, we will be ready! We believe in the one true church of Christ and that the Antichrist will be coming soon. We must do everything we can to prepare. Jesus wants us to put in order what we must to defend our life with a sword. We're in it for the long term and not immediate rewards."

"Really, a sword? Why not a gun or bomb?" Eve worried briefly that her contempt was showing through, but Mr. Carter did not appear to notice.

"The sword is metaphorical; we can use whatever weapon is required to win this battle against evil."

"One last thing if I may, do you spend much time in the city?"

He looked at her, wondering what kind of question that was, but her beauty and innocence won him over.

Before he answered her question, he wondered if he could ask one of his own.

"Absolutely, Mr. Carter, I would be happy to answer any question you have."

"Why aren't you married with babies? A woman with your looks and age should be home looking after her babies, not here talking to the likes of me."

Eve's eyes watered up, a trick she learned at a very young age, and she said, "I thought that would be my life, sir, but, alas, God needed my husband before we could have children and because of my devotion I never remarried."

He once again patted her hand and said, "My family and I like to stay to ourselves. We don't make it to no city unless our supplies are low, and then I send the boys to Detroit."

This was a waste of time. Eve abruptly stood up and said, "Mr. Carter, I apologize, I must end our meeting, I hope we can meet again, soon."

He stood up, gave her a once over, pausing ever so slightly, and then said "When you're ready to marry, again look me up. I have a couple sons that may take a liking to you, or maybe I will," He continued to inspect her, "You may be a little too old for my eldest son, he prefers them young, still in their teens, so he can train them correctly. My other son is not so choosy. He wouldn't mind that you're old, as long as you can still have children. Ordinarily, we trade our daughters with other like-minded militia groups so we can be sure that when they become women, they'll do as we say. It's important that women know their place in this world."

She smiled and walked to the door, quickly opening it before commenting that if he were so inclined, she would enjoy a walk with him.

He glanced at his watch and replied, "Seven o'clock tonight, outside the Convention center."

After that encounter, she needed a shower. She had never felt so unnerved around anyone in all her life. Eve was just happy she wasn't a weak-minded female that could fall into traps like that. She was sure if she were that sort of woman and ever stepped foot on their compound comprised of rickety trailers, that she would be locked in one, to be raped, impregnated, then worked until she died. She shuddered just thinking about it.

She got on her phone and sent a message to her dream team, "Tell me more about the Hutaree Militia, in particular, Carter's family."

Eve looked up at the clock and saw it was three o'clock. Her next interview was with members of the Aryan Nations. Once again, she hurried to her private car and headed back to the hotel and up to her room. She lay on the white down duvet and wished she could rest for a few minutes. She noticed her eyes closing so she jumped off the bed, opened the notebook to the third tab labeled "hot hot hot."

After a hurried shower, she slid into a tailored-to-fit black dress and the torturous Louboutin heels. A quick blow out and a flattening iron added a polished look to her hair and overall appearance. Eve refreshed her makeup, added Moscow-red lipstick. She knew without even checking that the jewelry would be minimal for this look. She swiftly swallowed a cup of coffee, thankful for the Keurig in her hotel room, but wishing for her beloved Starbucks, then left for the city convention center.

Chapter Nine

Ohio Militia Weapons Exchange

Eve's dream team managed to find Joshua Carter's mother-in-law, a member of the Ohio militia. Franklin made a trip to Ohio and arranged a clandestine meeting with her. The story she told was relayed back to Eve via email.

Joshua met his wife Marion when she was just fourteen years old on a weapons exchange trip with the Ohio militia. Marion's mother saw the way the older man looked at her little Mari and knew that he wanted her. Marion had brown hair that was bleached honey blonde from the sun, and stunning green eyes flecked with golden brown. They were truly a window to her soul.

Marion's father was a born salesman. In exchange for his daughter, he received several hand grenades, semi-automatics, and Joshua's favorite Browning Hi-Power. Joshua wavered for a moment over losing his favorite weapon but ultimately decided that this innocent young thing was worth the price. Marion's mother tried to prevent Joshua from taking her little girl, but her crying and sobbing about missing her baby just wore thin with Marion's father. He quickly grew tired of her pleas. He promised he would give her plenty more daughters, but when that did not stop the whining, he backhanded her and left her on the ground bleeding. He grabbed little Mari by the arm and dragged her, sobbing, to Joshua's truck. The Michigan man locked the doors and started down the long gravel driveway.

Her mother, lying in a pool of her own blood due to a badly broken nose, looked up as the truck pulled away. The last she ever saw of her little girl was her reflection in the side mirror looking back at her mother with tears streaming down her face. Mari's mother knew the life that was in store for her daughter, because it was the life she had with her husband, his brothers, and others in their compound.

It was not long before Joshua impregnated his young bride, and, as soon as that baby was born, he did it again. He was determined to get a son, but after two daughters he seemed disgusted by her. He abused Mari, both verbally and physically, blaming her for the lack of male offspring. Then he handed her off to his brothers for their amusement and pleasure and began to plan another visit to Ohio. He vaguely remembered Mari had a younger sister.

Eve could tell Mari was a fighter. The team discovered that Mari, behind the back of her abusive husband, had been spending a lot of time at the library. Despite lacking a formal education, she was quite literate. Eve's team had received from the library a list of the books Mari had been checking out. The general themes were natural herbs and pregnancy prevention, self-defense, and surviving rape.

The amount of pain Eve felt for this woman was overwhelming. Eve had a distant father, and a loving stepmother. She never had to experience being sold off like a commodity, or the abuse Mari suffered at the hands of this fanatical family. Eve vowed to somehow help her and her daughters.

She was expecting two Aryan Nation members to meet with her that afternoon, but what walked in the door were four Neanderthals, shaved heads and tattoo-laden, blue-eyed, blonde-haired brutes. They tried to intimidate her, to surround her and make her feel uncomfortable. That may have worked on Hutaree (undercover) Eve, but she would not pretend it had any effect on Aryan Nation (undercover) Eve.

"Gentleman, please sit down," she said in a very commanding voice. "We have a lot to discuss and not a lot of time to do it. First, I want to thank you and your leadership for taking the time to speak with me today. I hope that we can find this mutually beneficial and I would like to begin."

Eve picked up her notebook and started to read the first question when AN #1 said: "Wait, can't we just talk first, get to know each other?"

AN #2 uttered, "Yeah, yeah, that's right we want to get to know you," said in an unmistakably lecherous tone.

"Suuuure," replied Eve, "What do you boys want to talk about?"

AN #1 said in a very husky voice, "We want to know why you study terrorists. Do you like bad boys?"

Eve looked right at him and said, "Don't we all?" The men laughed.

AN boy # 3 said, "Why not go out with us this evening? We could show you a really great time."

"I would love to, but I have plans. Perhaps another time," Eve's refusal was spoken in a way so sultry that the men, rather, the boys, practically melted in their seats. She leaned forward, revealing just enough cleavage, and said in a voice barely above a whisper, "What are your thoughts on killing for fun?"

They collectively laughed, shifted a bit in their seats, and looked uncomfortable. Surely, she was making a joke. But she continued to look at them until AN#1 finally spoke up and said, "I have no problems with killing people that deserve it, especially people that invade my country. I am an American warrior. My family has been here for multiple generations. We are the true-blue blood of this country and we deserve to own it all." The others nodded their heads in agreement.

Eve just sat back and smiled. It was clear to her that the one that spoke was the leader and the others were sheep. They would be willing to do anything that he told them to do, so all she had to do was win over AN#1. Eve pulled out her phone and put on some music. Then, in a barely audible whisper, motioned them in conspiratorially, "Well, you see boys, I have this problem. Earlier, I met with a gentleman, and to call him a gentleman is being generous. First, he called me old, then told me I was fit for nothing but breeding and raising children. He, in fact, alluded to trapping me in his home with his sons and training me to be a good, submissive little wife." She looked straight at AN#1, "Unfortunately, "I'm far away from my brothers and have no one to stand up for me."

This riled the men, as she knew it would. They could barely sit in their seats. They were so angry. They would not stand for some beast of a man to speak like this to a beautiful Aryan woman such as she without serious repercussions.

"If you think you can defend my honor, the man is Mr. Carter, and he offered to meet me outside the convention center at seven o'clock this evening. I insisted that I had other plans that were not breakable, but he threatened to hunt me down and hurt me if I do not show up." She held up a photo to show them what Mr. Carter looked like.

The four forcefully agreed to help and indicated with various words and gestures that they would protect her honor and make sure that Carter did not get close to her. She stood, thanked them, and said she hoped to see them again soon. Eve thanked them again for being brothers to her as she knew they would be and gave them each a peck on the cheek on their way out the door.

Once the boys left, Eve turned down the music and did a sweep of the room to make sure she did not leave anything behind. She had to return to the hotel to get ready for her date with Campbell Greene. On the drive back, she thought about the meetings today and predicted the meetings she would have tomorrow. She knew right away the Hutaree group would not be valuable. They lacked creativity and money. Figuring out a way to get them out of the picture, she felt, was quite ingenious. Teaming up with the Aryan Nation boys in this act would bind them to her. They were easy to manipulate and could be useful in the future. Campbell was her undeniable favorite of the day.

After scrubbing off the makeup and brushing out her hair, she dressed in a simple, white, flowing and somewhat sheer dress with sandals. Eve had received a text from Campbell earlier that day and they agreed to meet at The Loving Hut restaurant.

When her car pulled up to the restaurant, Campbell was there waiting. He had on the same dark jeans, but his t-shirt had changed. This one said, "TAKE CARE OF THINGS THAT MATTER TO YOU" with the Earth as a backdrop. She could not help but think that she was the reason he picked that one.

As soon she was out of the car, he reached for her hand, gave her a big toothy smile, and they walked inside. The restaurant looked small from the outside. Inside it was like a cross between a home dining room, with comfy tables and shelves full of books, and a deli with full view of the food prep area. The first thing Eve noticed when entering were the plaques of famous vegetarian or vegan celebrities. Alas, they also felt the need to add framed motivational quotes, something she despised.

Campbell ordered a Seitan Panini and she a pumpkin chili. The kitchen was visible from the table, so Campbell and Eve were able to watch them prepare their food. They uncorked and consumed a pricey Chardonnay, laughing and enjoying each other like old friends. At one point during dinner, Eve received a text from a private number, with one simple word, "Done." She smiled a half-smile and looked up at Campbell, "Dessert?"

When they finished and left the restaurant, her car was waiting, and her driver was holding the door open. Eve looked around and back into the restaurant and wondered, "How did he know we were leaving?" Their table was not visible from the outside so the driver could not have seen them getting up to leave. She shrugged it off, gave Campbell a hug and thanked him for a wonderful evening. She slipped into the car and said to the driver, "Impeccable timing." His response was a simple, "Thank you ma'am," and they were off.

Chapter Ten

Boys Night Out

It was early evening in Cincinnati and, although he was in the heart of downtown, Joshua felt quite safe. He glanced down at his watch, "It's nearly time, if she is late, I will definitely have to punish her." The idea thrilled him. A car sped past him in such a hurry that Joshua wondered if something was happening and looked about. The street was active with cars and city buses. There were a few pedestrians about. The lanyards gave it away that many were conference attendees. A stray dog knocked over a dented trashcan nearby and started sniffing around in the spilled contents.

There was graffiti on nearby buildings, and a few panhandlers on the corner. He also spotted a few scantily clad ladies parading up and down a side street.

Joshua found the noises of the city off-putting and preferred his country homestead. Sirens, horns honking, breaks squealing and the whooshing of cars as they passed just drove home the idea of how insignificant he was, outside of his Hutaree family.

Matt, AN #1, was the first of the Aryan Nation brothers to see Joshua, and as planned he walked up to the man and said, "Are you, Mr. Carter?" Carter looked a little nervous when the skinhead approached him, but his nervousness disappeared when the man said, "Dr. Nicole told me to tell you she'd be a little late due to an unscheduled dinner and asked would you like to meet her at the Bistro on Elm Street," he pointed, "Around the corner, in twenty minutes."

Joshua thanked the young man and watched him head east. He was excited. He really liked the look of this woman and believed taming her would be thrilling. He had an idea. Joshua pulled out his phone and dialed his brother, Wallace.

"Wallace, I have found Mari's replacement." Joshua had to cover one ear with his hand and push his cellphone as close to his ear as possible to hear his brother's response.

Wallace cackled, "A new wife, eh little brother? What's she like?"

"This is an educated one, an academic. She is some

kind of doctor-not the kind at the hospital. She could teach the kids. But there's a catch, she will not come willingly."

Wallace caught the excitement in Joshua's voice and started to feel it himself, "Road trip?"

"Yeah, I want you to bring the van, get Marty and Jeb and be here tomorrow evening. Bring the tape, ropes, taser, everything, she is not going to be as easy to get as your wife was when we brought her home," Joshua's excitement doubled at the memory of her frantic struggle. He anticipated the fight that Dr. Mathers would give them and licked his lips.

"That may be true little brother, but my Emily has not let me down, I have three sons thanks to that filly. Jeb's new wife seems to be stirring up some trouble. I think he released her too soon. She's a beauty but her constant crying annoys everyone."

Joshua sighed, his youngest brother, fifty-four-year-old Jeb, really liked the fighters. His latest wife was a twenty-two-year-old who refused to see what was for her own good. "We're going to have to get her trained fast or get rid of her. We don't need any attention on us right now."

Joshua was still talking to Wallace when he turned right on Elm and realized the neighborhood had changed dramatically from the area nearer the conference center. There was litter strewn across the sidewalk, and the smell of rotting garbage and animal waste was overwhelming. There was a large cardboard box on the sidewalk, soaked from early afternoon rain, which looked to be once home to a vagrant, due to the grimy blanket on the ground nearby. There was a sign on the wall of a building that at one time said, "Loading Area"; however, some individual thought it would be clever to add the word "butt" to the beginning of the phrase. "Disgusting," Carter thought as he read it.

The streetlights did not fully penetrate the darkness and left large areas unilluminated. He feared he could be heading into a dangerous part of town, but then he thought about his beautiful, sweet, Nicole. If she was not afraid to be there, then neither would he be. Regrettably, for him, it was just then that three guys came out of nowhere and surrounded him. He dropped his phone and the glass cracked. He could faintly hear Wallace calling his name. Joshua reached in his pocket, threw his wallet as far as he could, hoping to prevent a beating, but the men ignored the wallet.

One of the thugs struck him in the face with his fist, a blow so hard his neck cracked as his face flew to the side, and he was sure one or two teeth had fallen to the ground. He looked over at the one of the others in time to have a baseball bat make contact with his knee, dropping him onto the cement. The bat was raised once again, but this time it met with the back of Mr. Carter's head. He saw stars and was hoping to lose consciousness when one of the men leaned in and said with a snicker, "Dr. Nicole wanted us to tell you she was so happy to have met you, and she's the reason you are now going to die."

He pulled out a knife and stabbed Joshua repeatedly, until his wails of pain ceased, and his body no longer moved. The blood that rapidly pooled out from under

Joshua's body threatened to surround them, so they backed away, but continued to watch, not wanting this surreal moment to end.

They had taken a life, a first for all of them. They glanced from one another and back to the dying man on the street.

Wallace was still on the line and could hear the cries as the men beat his little brother. He heard the name, Dr. Nicole. Was this the woman they were supposed to be kidnapping? He yelled out to Joshua, repeating his name over and over until the line went dead. He feared the worst. Fucking women, his brother was likely dead because of a goddamn woman. He threw down the phone and turned to see his wife, Emily, cooking dinner. Wallace reached out and grabbed her by the hair, causing her to spill boiling water all over the stove and on her clothes. He dragged her out the door and threw her onto the ground. "Get the family together, start with Jeb, and hurry," offering up a kick for motivation.

When the Aryan Nation boys were sure Joshua was good and dead, Matt wiped his knife on the dead man's shirt and casually pulled out his phone. One of his Aryan Nation buddies, Marky, had videotaped the entire thing and posted it to the dark web. They knew they would make a few dollars from the video. There were always sickos out there willing to pay to watch an actual killing, and with hackers like the infamous BobD, he knew they could do it without ever being identified.

"Case of beer and watch some TV?" Matt suggested.

"Sure," Bobby said, "But I ain't got no money."

Matt walked to where Joshua had thrown his wallet. Fortunately for them, he wasn't a fan of banks and preferred to use cash. "We have plenty of money, let's hire a girl to go down on us while we watch."

His friends hooted and hollered. They were hyped up from committing their first murder and wanted to cause more trouble. As they started walking toward their hotel one put his hands in his front pockets and stepped up his pace, "Come on guys, the hotel is quite a hike, and I'm getting fucking cold."

One of his buddies laughed and said, "I can grab the old man's jacket for you, he won't be needing it no more."

"No thanks, dude, let's just get there. Who's calling the girl?"

Marky looked down at the bloody sneaker prints he left with each step, "Oh shit, I have to get some new shoes, this day is starting to suck. This girl better do one hell of a job to make up for me having to toss my sneaks."

Bobby was tired of Marky's whining, "Listen man, you can't get down. We'll buy new shoes for all of us. We just saved that beautiful doctor from that dirty old fuck. We're heroes."

"It feels pretty God damn good to be heroes. My dad would be so proud if he were alive right now."

Marky sighed, "Yeah, mine too."

Chapter Eleven

Conference Day Two

Eve woke with a frown on her face and a pain behind her left eye. She would be skipping the gym. When she sat up in bed the world started spinning and she had to rush to the bathroom before the need to vomit took over. It surprised her how much better she felt having relieved herself of her stomach contents. After grabbing a hotel robe from behind the door, she wrapped herself up and hurried over to start a cup of coffee. Today's costume, as she was now thinking of them, was a modest, simple dress, fitted, but with a collar and sleeves. The shoes were simple, nude flats. She would wear no jewelry, no makeup, hair shiny and clean, straightened and flowing down her back. Her first interview was set for eight o'clock in the morning. After the previous day's exhausting back and forth, Eve decided to pack a bag and bring everything she would need with her to the convention center.

Still feeling ill, Eve went down to the hotel restaurant and ordered herself some breakfast. She kept her head down for fear someone would try to engage her in conversation and concentrated on eating her food and planning her day. When she was done with her breakfast, she sent a quick text to her driver and walked outside the hotel to wait. The sunlight was blinding. "A pair of sunglasses would make her day so much nicer," Eve said to herself. It was only a matter of minutes until her driver pulled up in a limo and she relaxed in the back for the short trip to the convention center.

She asked her team to get a women's restroom near the conference room closed so she could use it as her own personal dressing room. Today was the final day of the IDEC conference. She had to wrap up the interviews and set the next part of the plan in place.

The artwork in the room had changed again. This morning the colors reminded Eve of a warm blast of dazzling sunlight on a safari, water droplets on tall willowy grasses, and glistening golden prairie lands. The ambiance was one of new growth, healing, and a place of plenty.

Eve's headache was not improving, she refused to acknowledge what it really was, wine-infused dehydration of the body, she was hungover. The credenza once again had bottles of water and after Eve downed five of them, she started to feel a little better, water-logged, but better. Eve heard a knock on the door, the first meeting was a husband and wife team from Jamaat al-Fuqura.

Elaine and Rafael walked in. Elaine was an elegant, imposing African woman in a traditional print dress and complementing head wrap; however, the wrap fitted her head tightly, in Muslim style, not the taller and flashier African way. Rafael was also in traditional clothing, but it did not look as elegant on him as it did on her. Even so, they made a striking couple and Dr. Mathers was looking forward to getting to know them.

Eve greeted them both and invited them to help themselves to the selection of beverages and continental breakfast items. They both politely declined and sat down, Rafael to Eve's right, and Elaine next to him on the other side.

After introductions Eve got down to business, "Tell me about your home." This first question served as an ice breaker and could be informative. She enjoyed hearing how people see their home relative to how others see it.

The couple lived in small trailer compound in southern Virginia, in Charlotte County. Rafael said he was trying to farm, but Elaine laughed and said it was more like a garden. They both laughed together, much like an inside joke that only the two of them could appreciate. Their posture was relaxed, and their eyes brightened as they shared with Eve little vignettes about their life together.

They called the land they shared with other al-Fuqura members a settlement, but Eve knew what it was. She had seen the photos. It was a small plot with several trailers, all in various states of decay and rot, looking much like SFH before they started building permanent structures and becoming a respectable village. To Elaine and Rafael, it was paradise. The two touched each other quite affectionately as they spoke. With slight smiles on their faces and an unfocused gaze, they told Eve about their home. Rafael said it was a place he could live in peace, pray and, smiling back at his wife, play in the garden. Elaine was a schoolteacher.

Eve shared with the couple her own upbringing in SFH and how important it was to the group to be self-sufficient. When Rafael asked her in what state she grew up, she suddenly realized her mistake. She had just told them Eve's home story, not Dr. Mathers. Now, come to think of it, Eve realized she had done the same thing yesterday when interviewing Greene and Carter. Bloody hell. She was pretty sure the boss had listening devices in the room and she would hear about it when she next saw SAC Lange. If he found out how many times, she had broken cover he would never let her go undercover again. Maybe that wouldn't be so bad. She muttered something about Oregon then looked at her notebook as if thinking about her next question.

When Eve asked them why they chose to isolate themselves, Rafael said the community wanted a simple life, free from the decadence of a godless society. They responded with sadness to her next question about the surrounding neighbors' attitude toward them. "Prior to

9/11 we got along with our Christian neighbors, but now it seems like we're the after party. Men in rickety trucks come out and throw Molotov cocktails, start fires, scare our children. We have even had a few outsiders show up with rifles and fire them at the trailers. Guards are needed 24/7."

Eve knew that this couple, and the Jamaat al-Fuqura organization, were neither innocent nor helpless, but she could not call them out. She feigned concern for the small tribe and ask how they protected themselves.

Rafael's body language changed immediately. He became more upright and alert, his eyes glancing around the room and then, looking directly at Eve he said proudly, "We are well equipped to protect our family and our way of life. We will not be someone's pastime, a target of hostility or anger. When we are attacked, we have, and will continue to fight back."

Eve pushed, "Historically, the Jamaat al-Fuqura are known to commit fire bombings and murders. Do the al-Fuqura feel that the only way they can live peacefully is to promote violence and death?" She hoped that by referring to the organization and not to them personally they'ld feel free to give a more honest response.

Rafael's brow wrinkled, and with his jaw set, he said in a raised voice, "We are Muslims of America. Our village, and the 21 other villages in the US, are prepared to fight for Allah, our family, and our beliefs, regardless of the cost." He then stood up, "We must go, thank you for your interest. As-Salaam-Alaikum."

Eve had noticed the moment Rafael's fight or flight reflex kicked in and wanted to calm the situation. She stood up, thanked them both and replied "Wa-Alai-kum-Salaam." The meeting was over. Rafael opened the door and they both left, without Elaine saying a word.

They did not like her last two questions. Rafael's response, his obvious suspicion as the interview progressed, his defensive posture, and his peacocking made Eve feel sure their compound was well stocked with weapons. They were likely one disagreement away from starting a micro-war.

After the couple left, she grabbed a coffee and a donut. The sugary-sweet piece of goodness was calling out for her during the whole meeting and she was sure her desire to gobble one (or two) was what had distracted her enough to accidentally tell the couple her real background. She glanced down at her watch. Plenty of time to eat, change, and get ready for interview number two.

Eve finished the donut in three bites and grabbed another. She closed her eyes, inhaled the aroma of fresh coffee, and thought to herself, "On a scale of one to ten, what were the chances that they believed I'm really an author?" She knew the interview had not gone well, but with only two meetings left, this was not the time to lose her composure. Eve was supposed to be making connections that would benefit the FBI long term. They had invested a lot of money, time and resources to make sure this mission was successful. She couldn't mess it up any more than she already had.

For the next interview, there was no change of clothing, hairstyle, or makeup. Eve had become so accustomed to the quick change, that she was surprised at her own sense of relief. She knew she had to step it up and was glad for the down time to mentally prepare.

They were known as the New York Four. They had all been arrested on weapons charges after they had attempted to blow up a few military installations, but their lawyer was very good. He managed to sell some of the jury members on entrapment by the FBI and the jury could not reach an agreement. It ended in a mistrial and the four walked. Eve knew this case intimately. She had listened to the recordings, had watched the videos, and she knew full well that the "poor African American persecuted by the feds" was nothing more than a trumped-up defense. One of the videos in evidence clearly showed the four men exiting their car, each with a backpack holding a bomb, placing them in two different cars outside of a synagogue, and then returning to their own car before the FBI stepped in. The informant may have offered them money, but the four were willing to kill, and the video evidence was undeniable.

Payton, William, Jackson, and Jim walked in. One of the men, Payton, was wearing a taqiyahs, the short, rounded skullcap traditionally worn by Muslim men. Once they were all seated at the table, Eve introduced herself as Dr. Nicole Mathers and reminded them that this interview was for a book that would allow those charged with acts of terrorism to tell their side of the story. She also shared with them statistics from her previous book, *The American Terrorist*. She explained that the majority of U.S. citizens charged with terrorism are educated, come from a middle or upper-class background, and are Caucasian.

During her little speech, she noticed the men becoming more comfortable. Eve chose to highlight select items from her book that were true and would give the four a reason to believe she was on their side. She suggested that this was an opportunity for them to change her readers' opinions about groups such as theirs. She then asked each of them to share, if comfortable, something that they felt readers would like to know about them.

Jim was the first to chime in, "I knew it was da white guys an' Arabs doing all dat terrorism, and probly the Jews too, did you find any Jew terrorists? I know'dey do it fo money, dat's all dey care about, money. See, we are good, faithful Muslim men! We just tryin' a live a good life and dem FBI took one look at us, poor, black men, an' dey decided to make us examples. They thought we was too poor to fight it." The other three nodded their heads in agreement as Jim spoke.

Jim, a painfully illiterate man with a criminal record that spanned his life, was trying to convince Dr. Mathers that he was innocent. Eve couldn't help but think of him as silly. She recognized the look and attitude of an overly confident man. He had his arms crossed, a sneer on his face, hair trimmed close to the head, and a look in his eyes saying he would gladly take you out and shoot you if you didn't agree with him. The one known as Payton did not seem to fit in with the other three. Where they were openly hostile and defensive to the point of offense, he was calm and appeared to be absorbing it all.

"What about you, Payton, what are your thoughts on what you four experienced?"

"Well, Ms. Mathers, I mean Dr. Mathers, sorry, no disrespect meant. I agree with Jim, that experience almost ruined our lives, and to me, this was the wakeup call I needed. Now I'm married, have three lovely daughters and am studying to be an Iman. Too much of my life I spent hating others and thinking how unfair it was that the opportunities were available for them, but not me." He pulled out his phone and showed Eve his home screen with three beautiful teenage girls and a smiling happy wife. Pride and happiness were reflected in his eyes. "Now I know life is what you make it."

"Yo, P, why you even agree to come here an' talk to the doctor? We ain't seen you in years and now you sayin' you too good for us, man." That was William, a skinny, tall man, so stringy and flexible that he could fit through slats in a fence.

Eve fought the desire to react. She knew that she could kick the shit out of William, but there was no need to go there.

"Bill, you know he didn't mean it like that, cut the man some slack. He's just all up in his religion family, livin' da life we all wisht we had. Be cool. Payton, you know you're still one of us." Jim looked right at Payton when he said that, the last part sounding like a threat.

"Sure Jim, I hear you." Then Payton turned to Bill, "I am here for the same reason we're all here, the ten thousand dollars we each receive for doing the interviews. I have three daughters who will go to college and that money will help."

The only one that had not said a word during this whole conversation was Jackson. While Jim was clearly the leader, Jackson had the most threatening appearance.

He had piercing blue eyes, high cheekbones, chiseled jaw, and there was no hiding that ripped, tattooed body under the fitted, buttoned down white shirt. Eve realized she was staring and quickly got up from the table, walked briskly to the credenza, and made a cup of coffee.

As the Keurig brewed her single cup, she turned and looked at the group. Jim, Payton, and Bill started sharing updates, but when she glanced at Jackson, she saw him staring right at her. His gaze was so intense that she grabbed the mug from the still brewing machine, spilling half the cup all over the counter, onto herself, and onto the carpeted floor. She heard a deep chuckle behind her, and though she had not yet heard him speak, she knew it was Jackson. She was sure he could read her mind.

Eve grabbed a platter of cookies, dropped them onto the table and sat back down, then realized that she had left her mug of coffee. Jackson stood up, went over and picked up her coffee, and placed it in front of her. Bloody hell, he smelled good, like soap, leather, and sandalwood. She inhaled deeply and said, "Thank you."

She took a sip of coffee and was relieved it wasn't too hot to drink. She drank some more, regaining her composure. She watched Bill take a handful of cookies and start to devour them. Bill, probably the skinniest man on this God damn planet, was eating as if he didn't have a calorie care in the world. She knew she didn't like the man, and this just confirmed it. When Eve felt composed enough to speak, she leaned forward and said "Jackson, I have a question for you. If you could do it all over again, would you?"

"Well, Nicole, if I give you an honest answer what will I get in return?"

She noted his use of her first name and pretended she didn't understand the innuendo, "Well, Jackson, as was already pointed out (glancing at Payton) you will be rewarded for your time and honesty as soon as this interview is over."

"Well then if I were to be honest, I would say the only thing I would change would be to kill the informant. He set us up."

Eve knew the informant died last year in a car accident, but she wasn't inclined to share that just yet. "So, you would have gone ahead with the missiles, the bombings?"

He shrugged, "We'll never know, will we?"

"Is there anything else you would like to share with me?" She asked him.

He smiled so wide his overly bright white teeth almost took over his face, and he said, "Meet me for a drink tonight and I will share anything you want."

The sexual connotations were not missed by anyone, but it was her response that shocked them all, "Sure, let's meet at nine, I have an early flight and can't be out late." She read the looks on the faces of the other three men.

They were obviously thinking he had just propositioned the lady doctor and she had just accepted. She stood up and the others followed suit, shaking her hand as they departed. Payton included a slight, respectful bow, and Jackson gave her a kiss on the cheek. She felt her body tremble.

Bill grabbed another handful of cookies, and was

cramming them into his mouth, mumbling as he walked out, "Thanks for the money, doc."

After a few quick-paced walks around the room, Eve made her way to the ladies' room, reserved just for her. This last interview was just what she wanted, and her anticipation was painted all over her face. The casual greetings from strangers as she walked by were met with smiles and good days, rather than her typical ignore-them-and-maybe-they-will-go-away response.

Pale nude pumps, a floral print dress, straightened hair, simple makeup, and no jewelry, that was the costume for her last interview. It was with a father and two sons from Virginia. The father was a military veteran. When he joined the army, he was Adrian Scott, but by the time he departed he was Mahmoud Hussain. As soon as his tour of duty was over, Adrian returned to Afghanistan to train with al-Qaeda and when he returned home, he recruited ten men, two were his own children, to join him in Jihad against the American kafir. When their camp in Virginia was raided, Adrian and his boys managed to escape and had been living somewhere in the Middle East when Eve's/Dr. Mather's team found them and asked them to come to this interview.

When they walked into the meeting room, the American-born, Caucasian men were wearing the traditional, long, white, ankle-length loose robes known as thobes. It reminded Eve of the three wise men in school Christmas plays and she had to stifle a laugh. Their red-hued beards did little to hide their ethnicity but did illustrate the level of fanaticism she was likely to encounter during the interview.

She reached out her hand to shake theirs as they entered, but they did not respond with a handshake. What she received was a bow, similar to the one Payton displayed with her earlier. She did not return the bow, instead, she decided to sit down at the head of the table and allow them to sit where they felt most comfortable. She knew the lack of handshake was not personal to her but was the Muslim way. Nevertheless, it irritated her, and Eve knew she would have to work extra hard to make it through this interview without hurting someone.

When they sat down, their body language made it clear they did not want to be there any more than she did. The three were on the FBI wanted list and they feared capture if the FBI were anywhere near this conference. Eve started with a question for the father, "Adrian, what made you return to Afghanistan after you separated from the Army?"

His response was polite but curt, "Ma'am, please address me as Mahmoud or Mr. Hussain," and he then went on to explain:

"When I was stationed in Afghanistan, I felt a connection with the Afghan people, the way they came together to help each other out. It was beautiful. One time there was a man walking his young daughter to school. He had only one leg and had to walk with a crutch, and the path was not an easy one. The war was still going on all around them. Everyday bombs going off, yet he was always there and always with a smile on his face, greeting the soldiers and his people alike.

It was a daily occurrence, and when I was on guard duty, I would give his daughter a piece of candy or something special, like an MRE dessert ration. She would giggle, thank me, and run back to her daddy. I loved that little family, and then one day they were gone.

Several weeks later I saw the man, he was worn, like he had aged years in just a few weeks, and through an interpreter, I asked him about his daughter. It turned out that the little girl was not his, but in fact a neighbor's daughter, Tahani. Her father had been killed by soldiers and her mother was too afraid to leave the home. I told him that was sad news indeed, and that they were lucky to have a neighbor like him, I pulled out a lollipop that I had been holding on to in case I ran into them again and ask him to give it to the young miss when he saw her again. The man's face dropped as he explained that she was no longer with us: a drone took out her home, killing the little girl and her mother.

Later, I asked my superiors about the bombing. They said it was the home of an al-Qaeda leader. Apparently, the little girl's father was supposed to be an AQ leader, and our government did not know he was already dead. She paid for her father's sins, and her father was just trying to protect his home. I lost faith in my country when this happened.

When I got out of the service my country no longer cared what happened to me. I was without a job, had no skills that count in the civilian world, and no one cared. I remembered the neighbor and the risks he took for a dead man's daughter and I knew I had no other choice. I flew back over to the same village and lived in the bombed-out charred home of that little girl. The man, Abdullah Mahmoud Mohammod, taught me the ways of Islam and I trained at an AQ camp.

While I was there, I saw them for what they were, freedom fighters. First, they had to protect themselves from the Russian invasion, and then the Americans. I had been part of that invasion. I made it my mission, for little Tahani, to protect them, and make their cause, my cause."

His story was a sad one and Eve understood why he decided to go back and protect the villagers. But the minute he decided to kill American civilians, how was he any better than the people he hated? She kept those thoughts to herself and thanked him instead for sharing his story. She told him she understood his sadness.

Eve's next question was directed at the two sons. "Did either of you join the military?"

The older one responded "No, ma'am, my brother and I received our military training from our father and his veteran friends at the America Ninja Training Course near our camp. The ANTC became our home, we were there day and night. It was second only to our studies, both academic and religious."

"What is your school like," she asked the younger one.

"It's not really a school, ma'am, we're homeschooled by ladies at the camp."

Eve found them both to be well-spoken and well-mannered young men and told them so. They blushed and thanked her. "Do you regret not living a normal American schoolboy's life?"

"No, ma'am, so many others have fathers that go off to work, come home in the evenings and are too busy to even spend time with their children. We know, we have friends like that. Our father spends time with us every day, he tells us we are his priority. It is our job to protect our family, our mother and especially our little sisters. This sense of purpose gives us a focus and a path. While our friends are running from responsibilities and getting into trouble, we are training and preparing for war."

With that last part, Eve couldn't help but notice a kick under the table, and the younger son glaring at his brother before clamming up. Eve turned to the father, "Mr. Hussain, I cannot tell you how much I have enjoyed meeting you and your sons, and having just a small glimpse into your lives, Allah yusallmak."

Mr. Hussain thanked her for her time, complimented her Arabic, "ma' al-salāmah" gave her a quick bow, and ushered the boys out of the room.

That went so much better than she had expected. After a quick look at the time, Eve realized she had worked through lunch and was starving. She pulled out her phone and sent a text to Nadia, "Lunch?"

The reply was quick, "Yes."

Eve texted, "Plum Street Café in thirty?"

Nadia's reply, "Yes."

They arrived at almost the same time and found a

two-person table near the entrance. After they ordered and the server left their table, Eve asked Nadia, "Would you like to help me rescue a woman and her two daughters? It will most likely involve a firefight or two."

Nadia replied without hesitation, "Sure, when?"

"God," Eve thought, "I could really love this woman." She replied, "Tomorrow."

While Eve wolfed down her sandwich and Nadia picked at her salad, they made their plans. They would fly separately to Detroit and then rent a car. They could be at the compound by noon. Joshua's funeral wouldn't take place for at least a few days.

Because he had been murdered, extra time would be necessary for an autopsy; his body would have to be identified by a family member and taken back to Michigan. This provided Nadia and Eve plenty of time to prepare. Nadia said she had friends in Detroit that could hook them up with weapons, and whatever else they might need. After lunch, they left the restaurant separately with arrangements to meet in Detroit the next day.

Chapter Twelve

Sex in Cincinnati

When he walked into the lounge, Eve rolled her eyes in exasperation and thought, "Get the hell out of here. I have a meetup."

He could not read her mind. He swaggered over, "How you doin'?"

He had reverted to his cliché Jersey Italian accent. Was this the real Vic?

"Vic, get lost, I have a date."

He looked around and said, "I can be your date, baby."

When she gave him that look that he remembered all too well he said, "Relax, I just came over to check on you and to let you know what I found out about your friend, Joseph."

Now she was interested, but before he could continue Jackson approached them. Skipping introductions, Eve told Vic she would speak with him later and with a meaningful look, let him know he had to leave. He left.

Jackson sat down across from her. Oh my, he was sexy. "Take one for the team," crossed Eve's mind and she almost laughed out loud as that was exactly what she planned to do. She found it very hard to concentrate on what he was saying when all she really wanted to do was sit on his lap, wrap her legs around him, and kiss those sexy lips. "So which parent is responsible for those incredible blue eyes?" She asked.

"Is this for your new book, because it doesn't really fit with the earlier questions?" He said, with a twinkle in his eye.

"Sure, it does" she said, "I'm painting a human picture over what others just see as a terrorist. This book is about revealing the human side of people who commit acts considered terrorism."

Jackson sighed, and responded "Okay, sure, I'll buy it. My father. People say I look like him. I don't really remember. He died when I was young. My mother and I did what we could to make ends meet. Right before we met the FBI informant, Hussain, my mother was diagnosed with cancer." He paused and took a breath. His blue eyes locked onto Eve's green ones. "We had no way to pay for treatment. He offered us so much money, and I knew I could use it to save her. I know it was wrong, and that other people could die, but at that time all I cared about was saving my mother."

In Eve's mind, people charged with terrorism were bad people doing bad things. She could not believe how much the stories she had heard over the last two days had changed her perception. Really, how different were they from her? She was shocked at her inclination to sympathize, especially with this beautiful man in front of her. "Get a grip, Eve," she scolded herself. "A lot of people have bad childhoods. But not everyone resorts to terrorism. Stop feeling sorry for him and do your job!"

"Jackson, I'm really sorry to hear about your mother. How is she now?"

"She died while I was in jail waiting for my trial."

Eve reached out and took his hand, and once again forgetting her cover, she shared, "I lost my mother when I was very young, and I recently lost my step-mother, who I adored. I understand, Jackson. I really do, I would do anything to have her back."

A wine steward interrupted the moment and placed two wine glasses in front of them along with a Domaine du Comte Liger-Belair La Romanee, "Monsieur and Madam, compliments of Mr. Stallion."

Eve was sure the FBI would be picking up this tab, and by the way the sommelier was going on, she knew this bottle was expensive. He poured a little into the glass and handed it to Jackson.

Jackson put it up to his lips, allowed it roll onto his tongue, and swished it about, "Oh, what a marvelous pinot noir."

Not only was Eve impressed, but the sommelier was as well. He clicked his heels, thanked Jackson and poured a generous serving into each of their glasses.

Jackson picked up his glass and proposed a toast. "To the important things in life."

Eve touched his glass and then proceeded to down her wine like it was the house choice on derby day.

Jackson commented that the wine was a spectacular vintage, and likely cost $2,000 or more for the bottle.

Eve did the math, realized her glass was maybe worth $500, the swig itself $200-$400, and nearly gagged. She would have been happier with a twenty-dollar Moscato.

When the bottle was empty, and the conversation was not, she suggested they go upstairs. In her room, she immediately asserted control. She pushed Jackson against the wall, but he, in turn, picked her up and threw her on the bed. She wasn't going to let him win and kicked, scratched, mauled her way on top of him. Once that was accomplished, he seemed content to let her take the lead. She didn't really need or want to fight, as long as she was in control.

When Jackson woke, Eve was putting on her shoes. Her bags were packed, and she was about ready to go. He watched her walk back to the bed, appreciating the way she moved. She leaned over and kissed him, then picked up her bags and turned in the doorway, "Trust me. I know you'll have doubts about me, but in the end, please know I won't let you down." She took his Oakley's off the console table, slid them on, and walked out the door. Jackson closed his eyes and smiled, knowing he would get them back.

Eve had left Jackson reluctantly and now she was running behind. Vic had sent her a text early that morning suggesting she meet him for breakfast. She needed to hear what he had found out. When she arrived at the Sleepy Bee Café, Vic had a coffee waiting for her. She sat down, looking every bit as tired and hungover as she felt. The sunglasses helped. She had to keep up the Dr. Mathers illusion as long as she was in Cincinnati, so she had taken the time to fix her hair and she was once again wearing those damn heels. She really wanted to punch someone for making her get out of bed so early. Eve picked up the coffee without saying a word and took several sips. It was hot. Delicious. Perfect.

"Well? Why did you drag me out of bed so fucking early? What do you know about Joseph Carvallo?" She probed.

Vic shoved bacon into his mouth and washed it down with orange juice. Eve toyed with the idea of jabbing his fork into his eye. She pretended patience however, waiting for him to finish chewing. He didn't wait for that.

"He's no threat, in fact, he's one of yours." He arched an eyebrow at her, piece of bacon on his lip.

Eve turned her face away to hide her bewilderment, "Why would they send someone undercover and not tell me," she asked herself. She took another drink of her coffee and looked back at Vic, "Go on."

Vic took his time. He chewed on another piece of bacon and waved his coffee cup at a passing waitress.

Eve's pseudo-patience was all used up. She really wanted to kill him now. Her mind raced. So Carvallo wasn't an international arms dealer. Someone had created a false identity for this guy. She needed more details. "How did you find out? Who is he working with?" She had twenty more questions ready to fire at him. Vic interrupted her.

"I found out because I searched his room and found his passport."

Eve's voice raised a little higher, "It was just there waiting for someone to find it?"

"Of course not, it was in the safe."

"How did you..." She decided she didn't want that answer. "Did you learn anything else?"

"Yes. He had photos of you from before the conference. The real you. I think you were his target."

This was not good news, but Eve did not have time to reflect, she had a plane to catch and a woman to save.

Chapter Thirteen

A Trip to Michigan

Eve had promised herself that she would rescue Mari and her children from the Hutaree compound. She decided there was no better time than during Joshua Carter's funeral. In Detroit, Eve rented a car under an alias and headed to Adrian, Michigan. She arrived the day before the funeral and stayed at a rundown motel so she could canvas the area and study the habits of the Hutaree. The next day, she found herself facing armed men preventing her from entering the funeral location. Eve told them she was there to pay her respects to the family and allowed them to search her car. She was not worried that they would find her weapons. She had hidden them in a very safe place. Besides, these thugs were more interested in her cleavage than her threat potential.

Eve did not know that Joshua's brother Wallace had been on the phone when he was beaten to death. Nor did she know about the fact that her pseudonym had been shared as the one behind his death. When a strange, beautiful woman shows up at a funeral, people take note. They may have let her into the compound and seemed uninterested, but all the men were keeping their eyes on her.

She parked her rental car near the makeshift church and went inside. There was soft music playing in the background and some people spoke in hushed tones, while others sat in the uncomfortable looking wood benches and stared off. There was an overwhelming scent of fresh flowers and candles. Eve never felt at ease in places of worship. Religion was noticeably absent in her upbringing. If any of the SFH members believed in God, they did so privately.

Eve once asked her dad about heaven and hell, and if he believed in God. She would never forget his response. He did not put down believers, but he said it was something we had to come to terms with individually, and if religion brought comfort to people, he was in support of it. On the flip side, religion is often used to hurt people, and John said when this happens people become fanatic and the world is a scarier place. He could never have predicted 9/11, but he predicted the cause.

It was easy to spot Joshua's wife, Mari. She was

standing near the casket with her two children. Eve noticed that the grieving widow had eyes as dry as the New Mexico desert. "At least she isn't smiling." Eve thought as she walked over to pay her respects. Eve politely embraced Joshua's young widow and whispered, "The asshole is finally dead, are you ready to break out of this place?"

Mari was visibly startled by the words, but when she looked into the stranger's eyes, she knew that Eve was not making a joke. Mari simultaneously nodded her head and drew her daughters in closer as if saying "Them too."

Eve said, "All of you, meet me here tomorrow morning, six o'clock."

When Eve left, Wallace and Jeb drilled Mari. "Who was that woman? Why did she talk to you? What did she want?"

Mari had to think quickly. The stranger had not given her name. "She said she was the daughter of the storekeeper in town and that she had heard about Joshua's death. She wanted to check on his wife and daughters, that's all."

Jeb pulled Mari close, "Now you wouldn't be lying to me would you, young lady? 'Cause I would have no problem pulling down your pants and giving you a hell of a spanking."

Mari tried to pull away, stuttering in fear, "N- n-no, I'm n-n-n-not lying."

Jeb looked over at Wallace, "What do you think? Could that be the mysterious Dr. Nicole?

"It could be. How would I know? Let's keep an eye on her."

"We have more important things to worry about, like what we're going to do with this little beauty and her daughters." Jeb licked his lips and slid his hand up her front, lifting her dress and cupping her breast. He then leaned over and licked her face as Mari shuddered.

"Jeb, you have a wife; leave her be. I was thinking we should give her to Joshua's oldest son. As far as the daughters go, in a year or so, one each to our oldest boys."

"Mmmm." Jeb almost panted, "I wouldn't mind getting my hands on either one of those two beauties." If we started grooming the little things now, they will grow up to be proper wives. He had to grip down on Mari, she was struggling to get free and started to kick him. Jeb then released her, pulled his arms from around her, and shoved her face down onto the ground.

Mari started to crawl away, she was afraid they would kick her, or worse. Her nose was hurting, and her lip was cut. She had the metallic taste of blood in her mouth blood in her mouth.

Mari looked up, searching for her daughters. Emily, Mari's sister-in-law, was sheltering them for the scene, ensuring they had not heard, nor witnessed, their mother's abuse Mari tried to clean herself up before making her way to the girls. Emily mouthed, "Are you okay?" and Mari nodded.

The two men had moved on and lowered their voices so the women could not hear what they were saying. Mari took the opportunity to shoo the two girls over to their RV, which they would never again have to share with Joshua. She packed a small bag, just in case they were really going to escape. Selecting only the basic necessities, Mari hid the bag under the bed. None of it seemed real, the idea that they could escape this place, and it could be as early as tomorrow, made her body tingle and her heart beat faster. The pain she felt momentarily subsided.

Eve had checked into the rundown motel alone, and had been, to all appearances, Dr. Nicole Mathers. But now, at five in the morning, she was once again Eve, dressed in black and ready to blend in. Nadia had reached the hotel late that evening. She didn't bother checking in. The sun was hours from rising but they were both wide awake. The motel had a coffee maker in the room, thank goodness, but only enough grounds for two cups. Nadia was dressed in black as well, but her dark, exotic looks would never allow her to blend in here in this small mid-western town. While Eve was at the funeral the day before, Nadia had arranged for weapons and gear with her contacts in Detroit.

They made it to the compound right on time. Having parked their car out of sight, they were on foot when they came across the two men pulling guard duty. Eve took one; she sneaked up behind him as he smoked a cigarette and pointed a gun with an attached silencer to his head and pulled the trigger. He sagged against her and she lowered his lifeless body to the ground. Nadia quietly slit the throat of the other guard, letting him fall to the ground to bleed out as well. The dying guard stared up at her confused and sad, but the moment was fleeting, and then he was dead. Neither would admit that they had momentary feelings of guilt or remorse, what had to be done was done. They were professionals after all.

Eve did not want to scare Mari, so she approached the church alone. When she saw the young mother, she suppressed a gasp. Her face was bruised, eyes blackened, and lips swollen and scabbed, but there was hope in her face and a light in her eyes, that made it clear she wanted this. They could sneak out before light, but Eve thought, after seeing Mari's face and the abuse she experienced on a regular basis, the woman needed choices. She looked into Mari's eyes and said, "You have two options. We all leave together right now, or," handing Mari a handgun with a silencer, "You take revenge on those that hurt you before we leave."

Mari took the weapon. Her face was an unreadable mask, but Eve swore there was a flicker of glee in her eyes, and a slight curve of the lips.

Nadia suddenly appeared from the shadows. The girls and Mari were ready to flee, but Eve said, "She's with me. Tell the girls to hide in the woods with her. You and I have a few things to take care of."

The compound was made up of trailer homes, a few free-standing RVs and poorly constructed buildings, like the church. Mari walked like an automaton toward the nearest trailer with Eve close behind. Mari carefully opened the door. The door squeaked and the floor creaked, but the folks inside did not move. Wallace, Emily, and their two teenage sons were sound asleep. Mari went to the side of the bed and stood over the sleeping man. As she looked down at him, his words, "Give her to Joshua's oldest son and her daughters to their oldest boys." Played through her mind. She whispered, "There's nothing Christian about you," and she shot him, without hesitation, in the heart.

Even with the use of a silencer, the vibration generated by the bullet impacting his heart woke Emily. Her eyes grew wide as she first saw Eve, then Mari holding a gun. She struggled to get up and realized her husband lay dead, half on top of her. She raised terrified eyes to Mari and lifted her hand as if to fend off an attack she believed was coming. Mari dropped the gun to her side and put a finger to her lips to silence Emily. She then blew Emily a loving kiss and motioned Eve to leave the trailer. The two sons slept on.

In the adjacent RV, they found Jeb fast asleep, snoring quite loudly, and his young wife, Angie, wrapped up in a blanket, in a chair reading. She was startled when she heard the door open but visibly relaxed when she saw it was her sister-in-law. Mari motioned Angie to get over near Eve and proceeded to walk up to the sleeping man. She spoke louder this time, and with more confidence, "Fuck you." She then repeated the deadly act, shooting the sleeping Jeb in the heart. Mari then told Eve, "She's coming with us." Eve nodded. They hurried to the next RV, Mari taking the lead, Eve next, and then Jeb's young wife. They were not prepared for what was about to happen.

Not everyone in the compound was asleep. Wallace and Jeb, not taking any chances, had posted additional guards. The movement in the compound had been observed by one of the guards, Jeb's oldest son. He made his way unnoticed to the third RV and saw Mari go inside. She was holding a weapon in front of her and the lady from the funeral was standing behind her. He recognized his young stepmother holding the door, took aim, shot and killed her. Without missing a beat, the young man jumped over the newly dead body, and straight in to the RV. That's when he saw Mari, and once again he lifted his weapon, aimed, and shot. This time the bullet's target was her arm, causing her weapon to drop to the floor, leaving Mari wounded and unarmed

At the sound of the first round fired, Eve had sought cover inside the cramped RV, and steadied her own gun, pointed at the door. She saw Mari take the hit and aimed her weapon at the guard with the gun coming through the door. She fired a shot and watched him fall backwards onto the ground outside the RV. Eve then shot two men who had jumped from the rumpled covers on the cots inside the RV. Neither Eve nor the guard had silencers, so by now the entire compound was awake. Eve pushed Mari toward the door, "Get to the woods - find your girls!" Mari ran off into the woods.

Eve knew her own odds of survival were not good. She was trapped inside the RV and she could hear shouts and warnings coming from all sides. When Wallace's two sons woke and saw their father dead, they grabbed their rifles and stormed out of the RV in their underwear.

Eve peeked out from between the shabby mini-blinds and through the dirty windows. It was her against at least ten armed men. She couldn't be sure the women wouldn't try to kill her too. The chances of coming out of this alive were slim.

It was then when Eve started to reflect on her life choices and images of her father, Camilla, and her childhood home came to mind. That was when she saw Nadia step out of the woods like a berserker, with two IWI Tavor Israeli assault rifles in fully automatic fire mode. If Eve could stop time she would have at that precise moment. Nadia looked like a superhero. The sun was rising behind her, flooding the sky with flames of red orange and yellow. She and her weapons were silhouetted against the morning sky. Nadia was a bad ass woman ready to take on the small militia group single-handedly.

The image of Nadia and her weapons had a similar effect on the men who had stumbled out of their abodes, half awake, waving guns about against an unknown threat. When they saw her their jaws dropped and so did their weapons. Eve quickly moved among them, collecting their arms and separating the men from the women and children. Nadia kept her guns trained on the men as Eve personally asked each woman if she wanted to stay there or leave the compound. Three of the women begged Eve to please allow them to get their children and leave with her. The remaining four had male children in their twenties and did not want to leave them behind. Eve and Nadia herded the men into one of the cramped trailer homes and the women were recruited to help zip tie their wrists and ankles.

None of the women knew how to drive, so Nadia transported one carload full of women and children, and Eve ferried Mari, Emily, and Mari's two girls. Before they left, they gathered as much food as would be needed for a few days on the road, as well as personal belongings.

As they started to leave, Mari's youngest said: "What about Patty?" Eve looked over at Mari.

"Patty is her doll, she left it behind." Mari explained to Eve.

Eve put on the brakes. "Where is your dolly hiding?" The girl pointed to the church. Eve got out of the car, weapons in hand, and ran into the building to get the doll. Nadia, seeing this unfold from the other car, covered Eve. She knew whatever had caused Eve to stop so abruptly and risk her life must be of extreme importance. When she found out it was a doll, she was not amused.

It was still early when they started their twenty-two-hour drive from Adrian, Michigan to Tres Piedras, New Mexico. Eve knew that if she really wanted to give these women a chance, they would need a new identity and a place to live. She couldn't think of anywhere safer than Tres Piedras. Her father could protect them, help them with new identities, and the community could teach them the skills they would need to make it on their own.

Before the group traveled too far, it was imperative they apply first aid to Mari's gunshot wound. Applying pressure was a temporary fix but worked because the bullet had not pierced an artery. Mari had not noticed the pain at first. It had all happened so fast, and her adrenaline was so high that everything seemed like a dream. As they drove further from the compound, she looked down at her blood-spattered clothes and the pain and shock began to set in.

They stopped at a drug store a few towns away and Nadia went inside to buy some bandages, hydrogen peroxide, ibuprofen, and a case of water. When they made it to interstate 90, they pulled over and cleaned the bullet wound more thoroughly, wrapping Mari in blankets, dosing her with pain relievers and encouraging her to drink water and rest.

After fifteen straight hours of driving, they needed a break. They found a motel in Nebraska. It had a pool. None of the women nor the children had bathing suits, but they had shorts, t-shirts, bras and panties. There was no one to tell them not to. Eve and Nadia assured them that they would not allow anyone else into the pool area. With the happy sounds of children playing and splashing in the background, Eve took the opportunity to call her father and fill him in on the activities that led up to this road trip. She gave him an approximate arrival time and was relieved he did not ask her any questions.

While the Hutaree girls and their mothers splashed around in the pool, Emily took off to get something from the car. She returned with a few plastic cups and began arranging things on the table by the pool. She had commandeered some chips from her husband's stash and even had the foresight to snag a full bottle of rum. She handed it to Eve. "This isn't much of a thank-you present but know that it's heartfelt. You two saved our lives, and we will never be able to show you how thankful we are." Eve appreciated the words, but they also made her a little uncomfortable, so she gave Emily a polite nod, pulled out her phone, turned on some music, and the group of women celebrated their escape.

They arranged for two rooms, with Nadia and Eve split up. Eve vaguely remembered living in hotels as a child, but that memory was one of mixed emotions. The Hutaree girls enjoyed their new temporary home, jumping on the beds, begging their mothers to buy them snacks from the vending machines, and watching television.

When they arrived at the Tres Piedras community center the next morning, the welcoming party was lively. Music was playing and a potluck lunch was spread out on the picnic tables. They had clothes and toiletry items for the girls. Eve saw the Hutaree women, initially nervous, visibly relax. Dr. Marconi, the village physician, was there to check Mari's bullet wound. She complimented Nadia on her first-rate job of keeping it clean and infection free.

The community found the Hutaree women temporary living arrangements until more permanent homes could be established. Mari and her daughters would be staying at John's house, and Nadia was going to stay with them for a few days. Eve had to return to work and face her boss. When she introduced Nadia to her father, he gave Eve a look that she rightly interpreted as "Just a friend?" Eve rolled her eyes and nodded.

Chapter Fourteen

Debriefing, Part 1

Eve had an appointment with SAC Lange the next morning. She caught a last-minute flight to Atlanta then a red eye to Manhattan. When she arrived at the field office, Lange's assistant looked at the clock and told her to go on in. SAC Lange's office was far removed from the spartan décor seen in the rest of the building. There was a dark walnut bookcase lining the entire rear wall. In front of the wall was an aged leather sofa and two-toned, sheep's wool Houndstooth blanket draped over the arm. In front of the sofa was a coffee table, with more books and today's newspapers.

On a credenza were two antique clocks and a painting of an ancient manor house with children playing in the yard. There was a serving tray with a hammered copper carafe filled with water so chilled that condensation was forming on the exterior, as well as two small matching cups. Above the credenza was a large monitor. There was a door to an inner room, one Eve had never been privy to, and hoped one day to see. To the left of the door was a lovely old mahogany desk. On his desk were piles of books in no apparent order. A closed laptop sat in front of him, and manila folders were stacked in a mahogany inbox tray. Opposite his desk were two chairs, and Eve chose to sit in the one that gave her the best view of the room.

She would have preferred the sofa, not only to increase the distance between them, but in this case, when eve knew trouble was coming, she earned for the casualness the sofa and appreciated the surroundings lent to the environment. To the left, behind the desk, was a matching file cabinet and on top of the cabinet were two framed photos. One was a family portrait, including Lange, a woman, two girls, and a young son, all looking very smart and smiling for the camera. The other was a very young Lange in an Army uniform surrounded by soldiers in a desert somewhere. Eve did not know much about SAC Lange. She knew he did two tours in Iraq after 9/11, before joining the FBI, and she had heard he earned an MBA at some unheard-of school.

What made the biggest impression on Eve was not what he did have in his office, but rather, what was missing, the unpretentiousness of the space. There were no brag walls, no photos of him with famous people, no medals or trophies indicating his triumph or power, and no degrees or certificates, identifying for others his academic standing. He was obviously a man that wanted to be comfortable in the space where he spent hours and wanted to be reminded of happy moments in his life.

Eve continued to gaze around the room, assessing the man through his belongings, and thinking about what was in store for her. SAC Lange did not look up when she came into the room, nor did he acknowledge her when she sat down in front of him. He continued reading the file he held and then abruptly set it aside. He cleared his throat, leaned forward as if to speak, then sat back in his chair looking at her over the shortest stack of books. He leaned back, clasped his hands together and started to say something, paused, let out a sigh, then started again. He had learned from past experiences not to ask Eve open-ended questions. "Eve, are you satisfied with the outcome of the mission?"

Okay, Eve thought, this is not bad, "Yes, sir, quite satisfied." She planted a big smile on her face with the hopes that he would mirror her, and the meeting could come to an end.

"Let's do a cost-benefit analysis."

Eve slumped; she knew she was in trouble. "Well sir, I do not think we can really put a dollar amount on something..."

He held his hand up to stop her. "Let's start with the pre-mission expenditures."

He flipped through the binder until he found the

document and proceed to read down the list:

- Coach $200.00/hour x 20 hours, (cost included the clothes and accessories binder, with photos) – $4,000.00

- Clothes/accessories – $3,000.00

- Hair – $325.00

- Driver and Limo – $500.00/day x2 = $1,000.00

- Vic Stallion – $10,000.00

- Dream Team Costs: Salary (staff/interns) = $45,000.00

- *The Mindset of a Terrorist* (two academics, 30 days) – $30,000.00

- *The American Terrorist* (AI app, "BookBot" development) – $20,000.00

- Airfare (Eve) – $1,260.00 (round trip, 1st class)

- Hotel – Cincinnatian Hotel, 2 nights, $570.00

- Meals – $300.00 ($2,000 bottle of wine not included, agent pays)

- Vic Airfare – $520.00 (round trip)

- Vic Hotel – Cincinnatian Hotel, 2 nights, $570.00

- Vic Meals – $350.00," he glanced up at Eve, shook his head and then back down at the list,

- Driver (undercover FBI staff member) and Limo – $500/day x3 = $1500.00, and lastly,

- Payment to interviewees – (10K each: Hutaree – 1; al- Fuqura – 2; NY4 – 4; AN – 4; Am. Ninja – 3; ELF – 1) total = $150,000.

Based on this list the cost of this mission was $270,395.00, approximately a quarter of a million dollars. "Now Eve, tell me what we gained that would make that cost reasonable?"

Eve started with the relationship she had established with Vic Stallion. "Mr. Stallion, Vic, was an incredible find, sir. Without him this mission could never have happened," but then, remembering the $2000.00 bottle of wine, she added, "Despite the fact that he was doing this job under duress, he really came through for us, sir, for me, in particular." She realized she could not throw Vic under the bus. She needed him for future work, and besides, she kind of liked the man.

SAC Lange just nodded and said, "Continue." His face remained emotionless.

"I also formed connections with Sergei Bodrovi, the well-known Surface-to-Air missile representative, Ali Amin, a Lebanese-born Ukrainian arms dealer and Hezbollah operative, Leonid Minin, international arms trafficker from the Ukraine and Nadia Leah Katz, an Israeli weapons trainer. Of the four, I felt Nadia would be the most useful and socialized with her on two occasions while I was in Cincinnati. In all cases, I believe that reaching out to them in the future, under the guise of Dr. Mathers, of course, is not only possible, but in some cases will be expected."

At that point SAC Lange asked Eve how she would feel being alone with them. Eve remembered Sergei and the hug and shuddered. Ali was nice, and she would not mind meeting his brother. She reminded SAC Lange of his leadership position in Hezbollah. Then there was Leo, Mr. Minin, another lecher. She would just as soon kill him as share a meal with him.

"To be honest, sir, I could be alone in the room with all four of them, but there is a chance that two of them, Bodrovi and Minin, would not make it out alive."

"And why is that, Evelyn?"

She thought for a moment, glanced over at the photo of his two young daughters, and said, "Because it is my belief that no female would be safe around them. It would take all my willpower to be in their company and not respond to their advances in a less than favorable way."

"Well, let's hope we do not have to explore that option. In the meantime, I think we need to get you into a few anger management classes," he then proceeded to write some notes down on his pad. Eve tried to read his writing but had never mastered reading upside-down. Eve couldn't argue with her boss, but she didn't understand how forcing her to attend anger management would in any way change the fact that these degenerates used their power to take advantage of women. Their problems were somehow hers? Lange had it backwards.

"Let's move on to the terrorists, what are your thoughts

on the connections you made with them?"

She gave Lange her assessment of Campbell Greene. "While ELF is a leaderless organization, it is my belief that Campbell is an informal leader and that staying in touch with him, especially now, when the climate is such a hot topic, no pun intended, would be beneficial. It is my belief he would want to see Dr. Mathers again."

Lange ignored her attempt at humor. "What about the Hutaree militia, I heard things did not go well for the leader."

"This is true, sir. We put together known terrorists and weapons experts. It does not surprise me that there were not more incidents of that nature."

"And your involvement," he asked, looking directly at her."

"Absolutely none, sir." She stared back at him. Why do people think looking into a person's eyes makes it harder to lie? She had never had a problem doing it.

"And who's next?"

Her relationship with the Aryan Nations was one he would appreciate. "I believe," Eve said, "That I can infiltrate the AN organization without suspicion and any time over the next few years."

"Eve, I don't think you understand what we are discussing," he paused, "I am not quite sure you're cut out to work undercover."

That was it, the blow she was dreading. "But sir, I..."

"Stop, Eve. I don't want to hear excuses. You messed

up. The game simulation - you may as well have just shown them your FBI badge - you were obviously weapons trained. You shared your own childhood stories during several of the interviews. Let's not get started on your um...relationship with the NY4, or Carter's mysterious death."

Eve opened her mouth to say something, looked at him, and quickly shut it. "Eve, I know you mean well, and as far as "Taking one for the team," "I do not want any of my female agents to ever feel they have to compromise themselves like that, do I make myself clear?"

Eve nodded. The walls at the conference definitely had ears, at least in the interview rooms, and probably a few attendees in the vendors area were undercover. She knew it was her fault.

"I think it's wise that we finish up this debrief, and then consider some alternate positions for you that..." she opened her mouth again, but he continued, a little more forcefully, "Alternate positions for you that still allow you to nurture the relationships you made in Cincinnati. I have to make decisions based on what's best for the FBI, do you understand?"

Her internal mantra started, "Do not cry, do not cry... I'm a fucking FBI agent, I do NOT cry!" When she felt she could do so she spoke, "Yes, sir." She felt her eyes begin to fill. Was her career over? Would she be stuck behind a desk? She had ruined her relationship with her father and missed time with her stepmother trying to be a good agent, and now it was over, just like that.

SAC Lange was not heartless. In fact, in spite of the

fact that Eve could frustrate the hell out of him, he liked her, in particular, her realness. He could see she wasn't taking the debrief well and chose to save her further embarrassment. He stood and walked over to the credenza to get a glass of water. He took his time with his back to her, allowing Eve an opportunity to compose herself.

When he returned to his seat, he said, "I really have a lot on my plate today. How about we pick up again tomorrow morning, say, eight o'clock?" It sounded like a question, but Eve knew she was being dismissed. She wanted to protest but she also wanted to run.

Eve nodded, stood, shook his hand and thanked him. She was crushed, her careless mistakes may have ruined her career. Remaining at work would be impossible. Instead, she left the building and headed to the nearest coffee shop.

Chapter Fifteen

The Ambassador's Son

When she walked into Starbucks, Eve was surprised to see Franklin there, drinking a cup of something coffee-like, and staring at a laptop. She wondered, if she moved quickly enough, could she get by him without attracting his attention? She was not that lucky.

Franklin looked up as she went by and said, "Oh, hello Eve. Fancy seeing you here. Care to sit?"

"Uh…, I'm just getting a cup of coffee."

Franklin noticed something was off. "Eve, sit here," he pulled out a chair, "I will get you a coffee, grande Sumatra, black, right?"

Eve nodded while taking the seat and watched Franklin as he stood in line on her behalf. She wondered briefly how he knew her coffee preference. Surely, in his work as part of the dream team he hadn't come across her coffee preference... She continued to stare at him. At one point he looked back at her and she flashed a smile, but it was gone as soon as his back was turned. She really didn't know what to make of him.

They sat together and made small talk. He told her about growing up in England, and she shared her story about Tres Piedras and the recent death of her stepmother. Franklin thought to himself, "That must be what has made her so sad, how could I have missed that?" She abruptly changed the subject and started telling funny stories about the men at the conference, deepening her voice when mimicking the men and copying the good ol' boy accents.

He studied her: watching the way she managed to take a drink of coffee while laughing and just wiping her mouth as if she hadn't just made a mess. She told him about the 3D weapons simulations and going up against a female Israeli weapons expert. They both laughed at the idea that Dr. Mathers, academic researcher, almost kicked the Israeli's ass. Then Eve remembered how that was one of several fuckups that SAC Lange pointed out that made her unsuitable for undercover work. Her light-hearted manner changed as if a light switch had been flipped. It was like night and day, first she was laughing, then she was sad again.

Franklin tried to rewind the conversation and figure out at what point she lost her smile, but he could not quite place it. "Eve, let's go get a drink."

She agreed, stood up and headed toward the door. When she realized he was not immediately following, Eve turned around to see him mopping up spilled coffee, clumsily zipping up his computer bag and rushing to catch up to her. She really should switch to tall versus grande, less to spill if tipped over.

It was still rather early when they made it to O'Hara's. Franklin had picked it out. He ordered them both a Guinness and they sat down. After a couple more rounds, they were laughing and talking like old friends.

It must have been so great growing up in England, the ability to drink alcohol at an early age, having "mates." Eve held up her Guinness in a toast to all thing English.

"Oh, hell no, in America you have house parties, with kegs and red cups. In the UK we drink cider or vodka straight from the bottle and usually in a park while it inevitably rains. Besides, you guys are able to drive before we are. Hmmm... that may have something to do with the early alcohol consumption," he laughed.

Eve laughed too, "You're right, but the legal drinking age doesn't stop underage drinking." She didn't mention that she had never experienced house parties and drinking as a teenager.

"Growing up in England means frequent trips to Europe," she observed.

"Hah, that's because we have nothing fun to do in England! Did I mention it always rains? American teens say stuff like "Let's go to the beach this weekend! But in the UK the sea is cold all-year-round, and the snow we do get, barely covers the ground. In the states, at least in the north, you get crazy, amazing snow in the winter."

"I will give you that one, there is almost always snow in the mountains, and we even make snow in Taos and Santa Fe, for skiing."

"There is really no comparison, Eve, growing up in England was boring, and I missed out on several U.S. norms, like swimming pools, family camping, proms and school dances."

"But your food is wonderful, especially Haggis." Which was, in fact, perhaps the only British food she liked but was trying to be nice. She had grown up with a Mexican stepmother that loved to cook, after all. Eve liked her food spicy, and frankly, British food was the antithesis of spicy.

Franklin shook his head, "I don't know Eve, I don't think we can be friends anymore. You apparently have no taste in food if you like British cuisine. Give me American pizza, French fries, tacos, all the staples of the American culture." He reached down and grabbed a fry and threw it at her. She stole his beer and drank it down. At one point in the evening, Franklin started singing:

"Oh, Danny boy, the pipes, the pipes are calling
From glen to glen, and down the mountain side.
The summer's gone, and all the roses falling..."

His accent was spot on, and the rest of the bar joined him. They challenged another couple to a game of darts. Eve was good at darts. Franklin held his own and they managed to win. As the evening wore on and the crowd thinned, Eve thought to herself that this was the most fun she had in years. Eve thought to herself that this was the most fun she had in years and did not want the evening to end. She invited Franklin back to her place. When Eve went to the ladies' room he wasted no time typing her address into the Uber app on his phone. The driver was outside waiting as they exited the bar.

The only alcohol she had at her place was wine, so he uncorked a bottle and poured them each a glass. Eve asked Alexa to play some jazz, and sat back on the sofa, watching Franklin sway to the music while carrying a wwine glass in each hand. She shared with him story after story until she started repeating herself. Franklin did not seem to mind.

when Eve woke, she remembered very little about the previous evening. She looked down at her watch, 6:00 am, she had a few more minutes. That's when she noticed the glass of water and ibuprofen on the nightstand. She popped the pills, gulped down the water and pulled the covers up around them both. He was warm and she quickly fell back to sleep.

At seven in the morning the alarm went off and this time Eve woke to the smell of fresh coffee and bacon. She sat up in bed and Franklin was sitting at her table reading the newspaper. Eve stood up, grabbed her robe and walked first to the coffee pot, then to the table. She sat down, grabbed a slice of bacon and popped the whole thing in her mouth. She could not help but groan in pleasure at the taste, and then took a sip of the coffee.

She felt extremely content, and when she opened her mouth to say good morning to Franklin, he tucked in another piece of bacon and made a joke about him liking it when she groaned like that. They both laughed. She reached over to grab a section of the paper and they spent the next fifteen minutes quietly reading. She said she had to get in the shower. He gave her a kiss goodbye and said he would see her later at the office and left.

Thirty minutes later, Eve was out the door, heading to work. Thirty-five minutes after that, Franklin was back in her apartment. With her present, he had not been able to give the place a proper once over, but now he had all the time he needed. He noticed last night that her apartment was quite sparse. There was an almost dead aloe vera plant on her kitchen counter, and a really dead cactus on her living room coffee table. How do you kill a cactus? Reminder to self, do not procreate with Eve unless you can afford to hire a nanny.

He headed straight for her bedroom. The bedroom is one's personal space and if you really want to know more about a person you need to check out their bedroom, not the kitchen or living room. The only room comparable is the bathroom, and that only if they live alone. The first thing he did was lie on her unmade bed, face down, and inhale. The smell of Eve saturated the sheets, and it distracted him from his goal, but only momentarily. Knowledge was power and he wanted to learn all he could about Eve. There were not many personal items there. On top of her dresser was a collection of spare change, a book, he picked it up and read the cover, "The Shadow of You." It looked well-read. Franklin reached in his pocket, pulled out his phone, and took a photo, so he would remember to pick up a copy later.

He then opened her dresser drawers. The first one held her panties and boy did she have a collection, nearly all of them cotton. He found one pair of panties particularly interesting and after a pause he wadded them up and shoved them into his pocket. The next drawer held bras, he was not impressed with her large collection of sports bras, but thanks to her shopping trip funded by the FBI, she did have a couple sexy ones, that looked like they had never been worn.

At that point he lost interest in the dresser and moved on to her nightstand. On top were a lamp and a phone charger. Next, he searched her desk and bookshelves. Once again, nothing interesting.

As he made his way around the house it became very clear to him, Eve did not have a personal item in her whole apartment, at least nothing that would tell him more about the person he would soon own. As far as he could tell she did not have any jewelry, not a single piece. Odd. He would have to do something about that once they were married. She was his enigma, his paradox. While Franklin didn't have a lot of nice things to say about England, he was a fan of Sherlock Holmes. He was confident a woman with an apartment this clean had something to hide, and he was going to enjoy solving this mystery.

Franklin had spent most of his youth on an old country estate in Enford, a small village outside of Wiltshire, England, and three hours from London.

His father, an American Ambassador serving in Great Britain, did not earn a lot of money; however, a big advantage was free housing when living abroad. The title of Ambassador did have its perks, including mingling with the top leaders of foreign countries, and a nice pension upon retirement.

Old estates are beautiful. When you see them in photos or on the television, it's easy to feel envy for those living in such luxury. Sadly, the experience is less grand. The rooms are always cold, and damp. Wainscoting throughout the home helped achieve the look of wealth for the original homeowners, but the truth is the solid wooden panels were installed across the lower half of a room's walls to help keep the room warmer.

The floors creaked; there was no sneaking down to the kitchen for snacks, or into the house after staying out so late. His mother hated the musty smell and made heavy use of room fresheners. Franklin hated the chemical smell of the ever-present floral mists. They mingled with the musty smell and made things worse. He detested his home and the isolated village, and longed for a clean new apartment in a city, where everything one would need was close by, and he was not immediately distrusted due to his family's status or foreign citizenship.

When school was out, Franklin would accompany his father to London. As a young man he loved the energy of the city and the different food choices. It was so unlike his life in Enford, a small village whose claim to fame was that they were big enough to have not one, but two pubs, the Swan Inn and the Red Lion, implying that size does matter. At the age of ten his parents sent him to the Sherborne International boarding school, eight hours away, but he still spent his summers in Enford. On school breaks when his father's diplomatic duties lightened, Franklin and his father would spend their time hunting. Out there, in the wild, with a weapon and plenty of game to hunt and kill, just Franklin and his father, adventures like that were some of his favorite memories. The target of his hunt was dependent on the time of year. They tracked black and red grouse in the fall, pheasant and partridge in the winter and brown hare anytime. He lived for those moments. They were the only time he felt alive. Unfortunately, they did not happen often enough to keep him out of trouble.

With under a thousand residents, whatever happened in Enford was known by everyone in a matter of hours. His choice of friends were limited back at the estate, but he was quite popular with the girls. To them he was a wealthy dark foreigner and their chance to wed and get away from this rural existence. By the age of sixteen he had been seduced by or had seduced all of the girls in the village his age. Franklin was in a constant state of boredom. His infrequent trips to London helped liven things up, but inside he knew something was missing.

Franklin and his mates at Sherborne would push the limits of what was acceptable behavior and be sent to the headmaster's office. It was then that he would get the call from his father, who would remind Franklin of his duties as the son of an American Ambassador and a visitor in the country. It was the same song and dance...until one day he and his mates went too far, and he was expelled. When he returned to Enford his father hired a tutor that would show up twice a week to dole out and collect assignments.

Then one day, several weeks after his return to Enford, there was a knock on the door. It was a local village girl's father with his daughter in tow. He stated that his daughter was pregnant, and Franklin was the father. He insisted on an immediate marriage to protect the honor of his daughter. As he spoke of honor and responsibilities, the father's eyes roamed over their home and décor. Franklin and his father could almost see the dollar signs in the man's eyes.

Franklin's father told the man to come back in a week and they would settle matters then. Upon his return, Franklin's father handed the man a check. He told the gentleman that he had no proof that the child was Franklin's; rumors around the village professed the girl to have had several suitors, a piece of fiction Franklin and his father shared with their lawyer when he was hired to create the contract. If the man accepted the check for twenty-five thousand pounds and signed the contract, he was never to seek anything else from the family and the matter would be closed. If he did not agree, then DNA tests would have to be done, and there is always a chance that the child would not be Franklin's, and they would receive nothing. The family lawyer was there with the contract, handing it to the man, along with a pen to sign.

The man signed and took the check. Franklin's father, frustrated with his son for all the trouble he had caused, sent him back to the US to live with a relative, and to finish school in Boston. He just had one year of high school left to complete and was accepted to Boston University. There he obtained his BS degree in computer engineering before joining the FBI. Typically, the FBI likes to bring in people after they have a few years of work experience, but fortunately for Franklin, his father's position in the government meant he could leapfrog into a position with the bureau.

When Eve had first set foot off the elevator, so full of confidence and power, he knew he had to have her. She was the first interesting thing he had seen in years. The team had been briefed and had started working on her backstory before she showed up, so Franklin was somewhat aware of her history, but what was available was whitewashed and flat. It was as if she had no existence prior to entering the FBI. He could not find anything about her family, extended family, or her life outside the Bureau.

His interest wasn't merely investigatory. She was like a lioness, all beauty, intelligence and confidence, and he wanted her, all of her, body, mind, heart and soul. The back and forth banter they established during the mission was step one. Yesterday, the coffee shop and the pub, step two. The sex last night, a little sooner than he had expected, step three, and served to solidify his obsession.

Franklin knew he should step back and be patient, breaking into her apartment was cheating. Sherlock would not have needed to go that far. It was difficult to hold back when on a hunt with someone like Eve as the prize. Knowing her coffee preference at Starbucks was a major screw up and one he would not repeat.

Chapter Sixteen

Debriefing, Part 2

When Eve made it to headquarters, she felt reenergized and prepared to prove to SAC Lange that she was undercover-ready. Her confidence held firm as she stepped inside his office and saw him already hard at work

He looked up, motioned for her to sit down and said, "Good morning, Eve, I hope you slept well. Where were we?"

Eve's confidence was high, and she asked, "Sir, can we first discuss your comments that I am not ready for undercover?"

"What do you wish to say?"

"Well, Sir, this was a big mission. I had to memorize books, publications, basically learn a whole new field on a topic we covered in two sessions at Quantico. That was in addition to learning everything about my pseudonym and her life. I had to make others believe I was an academic, and dare I say, what a strange lot they are."

One side of his mouth lifted in a half-smile.

"In addition to all of that, sir, I had to learn the who's who in Arms trafficking, terrorism, and even learn the lingo. I think it's unfair to put all of this on me, expect me to be an expert in one month's time, and then be critical when I have a couple slip ups."

"Eve, you make some valid points and I will consider them more before discussing a move with you. Is that acceptable?"

"Yes, sir, thank you, sir."

"Now, Eve, we left off with the Jamaat al-Fuqura, how did that go?

Eve described to SAC Lange her interview with Jamaat al-Fuqura and why it did not end as expected; however, she felt that she had at least established credibility and could visit the compound if needed, maybe work on the relationship. She admitted to sharing her own personal past instead of Dr. Mather's past, but, in her defense, she believed it was the similar experiences that had made them both open up to her at all. She suggested that the FBI could alter Nicole's history to resemble Eve's actual past. If they could do that, it would make it easier for Eve/Nicole to, not only visit, but establish a long-term home with the cell.

She was equally convinced of her connections with the American Ninja cell and shared the story of the little girl and the neighbor. Eve let SAC Lange know that, based on what she learned, Adrian was less a threat than any of the others she met at the conference.

When it came time to talk about the NY4, Eve could not help but blush. She admitted the special relationship she had formed with Jackson, and that Payton had really cleaned up his act. As far as William "Bill" and Jim, she shrugged, "There was really nothing special about them, sir."

When she was finished, he told her to type up her own report, detailing everything they discussed and include anything she had left out that she felt might be relevant, and have it on his desk by Friday. That would give her plenty of time to work through whatever emotions she may be experiencing. He did believe that the connections she had created would cement her place at the convention next year. She would be able to continue to attend those conferences without raising suspicion and could gather more information. In his opinion, the mission was a marginal success.

Eve thanked him and started to leave his office, but stopped and turned around, "SAC, do you know an agent that goes by the name Joseph Carvallo? She studied him as he answered for any signs of a lie, but his "No" was delivered with a deadpan face. She left his office, walked straight to the elevator, down five floors, and when the doors opened, there was her dream team.

They greeted her with enthusiasm, and she spoke to them about the success of the mission. Bottom line, the boss was satisfied. Eve wanted to ask her team to investigate Carvallo, but she didn't feel like she knew them well enough for such a side project. She did know someone she could ask, but it would have to wait.

During her conversations with Joan, Harry, and Wennie, Eve kept glancing over at Franklin who was trying his hardest to appear as though he was working and had not noticed her.

When she at last said goodbye and pushed the elevator button to go up, he ran over to her and said, slightly out of breath, "Eve. Hi. Uhhh... can we meet for coffee later?"

"Sure Franklin, you have my number." At that moment the elevator doors opened, and she stepped inside. Hollywood could not have planned that any better.

Chapter Seventeen

Streets of NYC

As soon as Eve was outside and out of the range of the security cameras strategically located around the building, she made a phone call. "Hello, Dad." She started the conversation checking on the Hutaree women. Her father said, with an amused tone, that the Hutaree women would not leave him alone. "They are cooking and washing, one even tried to tidy up the bunker. I had to put my foot down. I think I've gained five pounds since they arrived." His words may have sounded like he was unhappy with the situation, but Eve knew her father was content, and grateful for the company.

Eve was glad to hear that the women were settling in, and that her father was pleasantly distracted. "What about Mari and her girls?"

"I let the little girls have your room, their mom sleeps on the sofa. Initially, the girls were so afraid they wouldn't go outside alone, but now they're playing with the village kids, even caught them on the tower across the street. I had to scare the living daylights out of them to make sure they don't repeat it. Do you remember what happened to Karl when you were kids?"

That was the most she had heard him talk in years. "Yes, Dad. I remember. Any sign of outsiders?"

"No, the whole village is keeping an eye out. They haven't had this much fun since the eighties when the feds would randomly show up," he laughed.

"And Nadia, when did she leave?"

His tone changed, "Well, honey, she didn't."

Hearing those words caused Eve to become concerned, "What do you mean she didn't leave, is she okay? Is she worried the Hutaree militia will show up? Do I need to come out there?"

"Calm down, Evie, it's nothing like that." He sighed. "You know how much I loved Camilla, right? She was the perfect companion and my best friend."

Eve paused, took a deep breath and responded with a "Yes..." wondering where this was heading.

"Well, she and I, you know..."

It took a moment. Her eyes grew wide and she cleared her throat, not quite knowing how to respond. It did not take her long to decide this was a good idea. Nadia would protect the village and keep her father happy. She thought Camilla would approve. Eve worried that this was a rebound for her father. Well, he needed someone. Why not Nadia? Who knows what Nadia was thinking. "Well dad, be careful not to make her mad, she is a bad ass, and she doesn't know who I work for, so keep that to yourself."

"I can take care of myself, and your secrets. Don't worry."

Eve shifted gears, "Dad, I have a problem. How well can you track down a Fed, an FBI agent, if I have a name, verified by a passport, which I know is not really reliable."

"It may take some time, but I can probably do it, what's his name?"

"Joseph Carvallo."

When she ended the call, Eve texted Nadia, "My dad?!"

The response was quick, not text, just a photo of Nadia and John, both smiling, with the Hutaree girls playing in the background. Eve responded with a smiley face emoji and put her phone away. She was not a fan of emojis or basically anything related to emotions, but her time as Dr. Nicole had left her wanting to pull a little of the doctor into her real life. Eve looked down at her Franco Sarto leather slip-on shoes and thought, "But not the heels."

As she headed to the Canal Street Station to catch

the subway home, she noticed a man watching her from across the street. For a minute, she thought it was Agent Carvallo, but then when she looked back, he was gone. Eve convinced herself that it was her imagination and continued walking, occasionally looking around, but not seeing anyone. She was happy to be back in her do-not-notice-me clothes. Eve passed an older lady dragging a buggy full of groceries and watched her struggle to get up a curb.

Eve showed her her badge and asked the lady to let her help. The woman looked as if someone told her she had won the lottery, her old body visibly relaxed and there was a new pep in her step as she walked next to Eve. It did not take her long to start chatting away, and made Eve regret, just a little, that she did not just walk past the woman. Six blocks later, a flight of stairs, and the woman was safely home, her cart and groceries intact.

After several words of thanks and an offer of coffee, as well as a phone number of the woman's successful nephew thrust into her hands, Eve left the woman, and continued on her way. She admired the lady, having the fortitude to walk a mile round trip to get a few groceries. The exercise was good for her. It wasn't long before Eve was almost run over by a large Dalmatian, one of six at the end of leashes held by a tired looking dog walker. He apologized to Eve and she petted the big puppy and assured him it was fine. Unfortunately, she did not have a habit of keeping treats in her pocket like her father, so a nice rub was all the dog would receive. It was enough to make all the other dogs want attention and it took Eve twenty minutes to show all of the dogs a bit of affection. By the time they continued on their way, the dogs and the walker looked much happier.

This route was one of her favorites. There were colorful food trucks, uniformed doormen tipping their hats to passing pedestrians, and plenty of shops with vibrant store front windows. Eve frequently ate food from the street venders. It was quick, and she could eat and walk, thus saving time.

The temptation was too much, and Eve stopped for a New York dog. When it came to hotdogs, she was a traditionalist. Her Big Apple dog was topped with a spicy brown mustard, sauerkraut with an extra kick of flavor from chili powder and beer. While she chowed down on the dog, she thought to herself how happy she was, and could not remember feeling this way for a long time. Her happiness was due to a number of things, her job was secure, her father was speaking with her again and he seemed to be enjoying life. For a moment her happiness was clouded by a thought of Camilla. She reminded herself that Camila would want her to be happy, and it was not as if Eve had forgotten her; quite the opposite.

She finished her dog and found that one napkin was not enough, so she used the bottom of her shirt, "Take this Samantha!" Eve said to no one in particular One person she did not miss was her style coach. It was shortly after her hot dog and self-reflection when she heard a scuffle in the corner bodega. She looked inside and saw a skinny drugged out kid threatening an older Chinese woman behind the counter. Eve walked inside and acted as if she had missed the exchange, but when the woman glanced her way Eve flashed her badge.

She grabbed a plastic bag and started filling it up with soup cans and walked up behind the man, still pretending to be clueless. Eve did not know the woman, but that did not stop her from acting as if they were old friends. "Oh, Mrs. Kim," making up a name and apologizing to herself for stereotyping, Mrs. Kim, I mean, could you get a more stereotypical Asian name than Kim? "You asked me to step in for you, so you could go to the doctors, would you mind just ringing me up, I had to get a couple cans of soup for the old man, and then I'll take over for a few hours."

It did not take Mrs. Kim long to understand what Eve was saying, and she played along, "Yes, Yes..." she grabbed the bag, pulled out the cans and scanned them, then returned them to the bag, "Thank you, I shall go to the doctor and return shortly." She rushed to the back and went into a back room, that happened to be a small apartment, and called the police.

Meanwhile the man just stood there, bewildered. Eve was now behind the counter with her bag of cans still in her hand, "How can I help you, sir?" She looked directly at the man. He straightened up in such a manner that she was reminded of her dog when he would puff himself up to defend his chew bone. Eve laughed at the thought and the man shuffled his feet and looked around the store, with bloodshot eyes and a frantic manner.

"Lady, I need some smokes." He looked around the store, again. "And a...," he wasn't sure what else to ask for, so he decided to go for it, he pulled out his gun and said, "And your money."

Eve did not hesitate or play around, she gripped her soup bag tightly and flung it at his head, "Bloody hell!" And down he went. Blood started pouring from what she was pretty sure was a dent in his head, to match the dent in one of her cans. Mrs. Kim was nowhere to be seen, and Eve heard sirens in the distance, so she quickly left the store and continued to the subway.

So maybe she had overreacted a little. There was a chance she could've talked him down, and maybe ended the encounter without violence, but it was so perfect, the bag in her hands, his head, how could she resist? Besides this would prevent him from doing this to anyone else, and, well, considering the size of the dent in his head, it may even stop him from having another criminal, or any other thought, ever again.

The lady with the cart, the dogs, the cans... what an interesting day. The sun was shining, and she was nearly at the station.

Eve had seen Joe, but only because he wanted to be seen. He wanted her to get anxious and sloppy and lead him to his actual target, her father. He had heard a rumor that a fellow agent was the daughter of Leonard Wilkins, one of the leaders of the Weatherman Underground. When he tracked down Dr. Nicole Mathers in Cincinnati at the arms conference and after speaking with her, he was pretty sure she was hiding something, and the blunder with the weapons simulation confirmed his suspecions.

He has been after Leonard since his Weathermen days. He had more than a hunch that Leonard, aka John, was also the dark web hacker, BobD. The name made it a little too easy. Bob Dylan's song had inspired the name for the Weatherman organization. Joe knew Eve was suspicious of him and had been checking his alias ever since they met at the conference. He was confident it would hold up under scrutiny.

It's damn near impossible to get the phone records of a fellow agent, but Joe had contacts outside of the FBI that, for a price, could do about anything. He had learned that she had only made two calls outside of the NYC area, both to a man named John. Eve was the right age to be Leonard's daughter. She had placed another call, less than an hour ago, to the same number. In both cases the calls did not last long enough to be traced. He wouldn't give up, Joe was confident that Eve would lead him to her father, and then he would take both of them down.

Chapter Eighteen

Moving On

Eve made plans to meet up with Vic for coffee in the morning. She didn't have an agenda; she just wanted to keep the relationship active. When he arrived, she was already sipping her black coffee. He waited ten minutes for the barista to finish his double espresso before joining her at the table. Eve studied him from across the room. Today he was wearing a nondescript suit and looked like every other businessman in lower Manhattan.

When he finally sat down, he reached out and took

her hands, "Eve, it is so good to see you."

She smiled and said to him, "And it's good to see you too, Vic." Surprising herself, she realized she meant it. She asked him how he was doing, and he announced that his oldest daughter, Maia, had just got accepted to Case Western. Eve didn't know he was married, let alone a father. He invited Eve to her upcoming graduation party, and she promised she would try to be there, although she had no plan to attend. The whole other people's family thing made her intensely uncomfortable.

"So, have you had a chance to see Jackson or the sexy Israeli lady?" He asked, a smirk on his face.

"You will not believe this, but the sexy Israeli lady is sleeping with my father!" Eve blurted. They both laughed over this, and she continued, "I left Jackson in the hotel room quite abruptly, thanks to your text. I don't expect to hear from him." The truth is she had heard from him. They had been carrying on a very intimate text relationship. However, that was something she would keep to herself.

"So, what have you learned about Joseph Carvallo, Eve?"

"Nothing yet, but I have the best hacker I know on it. By the way, I think I saw him a few weeks ago on my way to the station."

Vic got a concerned look on his face. Like Eve, his feelings toward her went beyond Informant/Agent. He truly considered her his friend. "Eve," he said, with sincerity in his voice, "I am only going to say this once, if you need help, just say the word."

She thanked him. She was not naïve enough to think she could navigate this situation alone.

When they stood up to leave, Vic asked Eve, "So what's next?"

Eve replied, "I think I'll head out west for a few days."

After a slight pause in the conversation Vic asked, "Eve, would you consider us friends?"

"That's an easy answer Vic, I consider you a good friend, why?"

"Eve, I think the same about you, and I believe I am a good judge of character." He paused, looked around, then continued. "If there is anything you need from me, anything I can get for you, you need only ask."

Eve wondered why Vic was pushing this point home. Twice now, in one conversation, he has alluded to her needing help and his ability to help.

Vic scribbled down an address, "When you're ready you can pick up whatever you need here."

Eve understood the enormity of what he was offering, and the kind of trust he was showing in her. She gave him a hug, a real hug, and thanked him.

What a conundrum he was, a man of the world. She thought back on his nervousness in the interrogation room, his boss look at the conference, and today, looking like a NYC businessman. Eve knew she should never underestimate the man. It would not surprise her if he ultimately worked for MI6. His skills were amazing, and the pedigree of his network would fit someone with the resources of the British Intelligence. Maybe she would make it to the graduation party after all.

The weather was perfect when she landed in Taos, her third visit this year, and Eve headed straight over to the rental company to rent the Jeep. With the top down and a fresh coffee in the cup holder, she was in a good frame of mind. Eve was also curious about her father's new relationship, and she was trying to decide how much of her professional life she should share with Nadia.

As she drove through the village, neighbors waved and smiled, and Eve immediately realized how much she missed the place. In fact, she did not realize how lonely she had been until this moment. Her whole life had been about keeping people at a distance. If someone asked who her closest friends were, she would say Vic, the arms dealer turned FBI informant, and Nadia, Israeli weapons instructor and her father's lover. It was clear to Eve that it might be time to share a little bit of herself and see where it led. Franklin popped into her head. Maybe her time as Dr. Mathers had a bigger impact on her than she realized.

Eve timed it just right; when she walked in the house, dinner was cooking and the clamor of many voices was, for the first time, quite inviting. Eve dropped her duffel bag just in time to have the Hutaree girls come up and wrap her in waist high hugs. They referred to her as Auntie Eve and she kind of liked it.

Mari walked toward her from the kitchen, wiping her hands on a dish towel. She gave Eve a quick hug and kiss on the cheek "It's so good to see you again, Eve."

"It's good to see you, Mari. It looks like everybody's doing well?"

"Oh yes," she looked around and smiled "We're all fitting in quite nicely."

"What about the others?"

"Well, one of them has a job at the community center and another is helping at the Farmers Market. We all agree our life has never been better and we owe it to you."

At that point Nadia walked out of the bedroom "Hey what about me?" They all laughed.

The little girls ran over to Auntie Nadia and asked her to play with them outside. Nadia told the little ones, "After dinner we can play."

Eve gave Nadia a hug and whispered, "Where's my father?"

"In his bunker, where else would he be?" She said, with wink, "Seba is down there too, you should go say hello to them both."

Eve agreed, grabbed an apple from the side table, and with her mouth full, she said, "I'll be back," and stepped outside. She made her way around the yard to the back, where she found the bunker door open. "Seba!" She called. Her old friend seemed to transform into a young pup when he heard her voice. He ran up the stairs and into her arms. As she carried the dog back down the stairs, she stroked his fur and whispered to him how much she had missed him and loved him. She was so full of love and happiness; all worry and tension was gone, and she felt transformed. It would not last.

Her father met her at the bottom of the stairs, looking very serious, and said "We need to talk."

Eve shut the door and settled herself into a chair, with Seba on her lap. Her father preceded to explain that he believed that agent Carvallo was the FBI agent that had been tracking him for the last twenty-some years, since his days as a Weatherman leader.

"So, what you're saying, dad, is that he's stalking me to get to you." She realized with a sickening sense of dread that she had not taken any precautions when she left the airport. She may have inadvertently led Carvallo straight there.

"Dad," she sounded panicked, "I think I messed up, what if he knows I'm here visiting you?"

"We will deal with that if it comes. Right now, let's go upstairs and have some dinner." Years of living on the run had steeled him to the fact that one day his past may catch up to him.

After dinner Eve went with Nadia and the girls to play in the yard. She could watch for any unusual activity. She decided it was time to learn their names. The oldest one was Jada, the younger, Rose. They were showing Nadia the new trick they had taught Seba when John came to the screen door. He opened it and handed Eve a coffee. "Thanks Dad," she kissed him on the cheek and together they watched the girls play in the yard, demonstrating that they had taught the dog how to fetch. Of course, Seba had known how to fetch since he was a pup, but they didn't spoil the moment by saying so, they just enjoyed the laughter of two little girls playing with a dog.

Eve missed Camilla and felt her presence everywhere, but she was happy that her father had this new extended family and by default, so did she. The girls' recruited Papa John to help them, and that gave Eve and Nadia a chance to talk privately.

Late the next day, Eve and her father headed back down to the bunker. Their conversation returned to one they had after Camilla's funeral. "Were you successful?" She asked him.

"Here it is," he showed her his computer screen, "The virus you requested that will take down PMI." He said the last bit with excitement and pride. He was satisfied with his programming and knew it would work, but his excitement and pride lay in the fact that his daughter was going to join him in taking down the insurance company that had dropped Camilla when she was diagnosed with diabetes.

In Camilla's memory, John and Eve would destroy the insurance company, a staple on Wall Street. Camilla would be alive today if she had the means to pay for her insulin, and John knew several in the village that had to choose between buying groceries and paying for prescriptions and doctor bills. He also knew the problem was only getting worse. "It's not just a Tres Piedras problem, it's a national problem," and John wanted to cause a disruption that would set the insurance company back years, and serve as a warning to other predatory companies.

Chapter Nineteen

Nadia Leah Katz

Nadia grew up in Israel during the transition from socialism to capitalism. The economy crashed in 1983 due to hyperinflation and external debt. As a result, the standard of living was half what it was in the western world. Eve's friend had grown up watching only one TV channel, PBS. There were no commercials on TV, but they did have government sponsored ads: how to save water, save electricity, road safety, workplace safety, unexploded ammunition safety and bomb awareness. Every public place had a bomb pit nearby, a four-feet deep hole in the ground with a heavy lid into which you could place a potential bomb and wait for the bomb squad. Most of the population drove a Subaru, (including Nadia's father) because that was the only Japanese car company that did not comply with the boycott.

Driving an American-made car was considered a status symbol. In school, one of Nadia's friends drove a Pontiac and he was the most popular boy in school. In Israel, anyone who had the means and was planning a trip abroad, became instantly popular. They could expect all their neighbors, friends and family to give them a shopping list for items they could not find in Israel. This was how Eve's father made his money, an unofficial import/export business.

Education was relatively good and cheap. Nadia was educated at the best schools available. In a place where it could take five years for a phone line to be installed, being a part of the supply chain meant that Nadia's father was in high demand. Hence, they enjoyed a lifestyle more like that of the upper-class, rather than that of the average businessman that he was. What looked like a fairytale from the outside felt more like a birdcage and Nadia was suffocating. As her father's wealth grew, so did her cloistered existence. She was not allowed the freedoms that her peers enjoyed. She was treated as if she were a fragile figurine.

Nadia would see her friends going off with boys, sneaking into the movie theater or recklessly roller skating with no fear of broken bones. Sure, most of their clothes were hand-me-downs and sometimes they went weeks without electricity, but they all seemed so happy and able to tackle adversity with a smile. She knew better than to admit how much she envied them. They would not understand.

On her thirteenth birthday, Nadia came down from her bedroom to stacks of beautifully wrapped gifts. Her mother was off somewhere else in the sprawling mansion and her father was in his office on the phone, setting up a transaction. Nadia quietly stuffed all her gifts into bags, not even curious as to what was inside the festive wrapping paper. She would donate them, *tzedakah*, to the poor. She dragged the bags outside and loaded them into her father's Subaru.

She was very excited and believed this would be the best birthday ever. As she walked back toward the house, she saw her mother watching her from a window. Both of her parents were waiting for her when she came inside. She breathlessly explained her plan. The sneer on her father's face was something she would never forget. He had no love for the poor or the needy, only himself and his family.

Her mother, looking proper and beautiful, stood silent as he berated Nadia for her childishness. She must grow up, appreciate what she had. Did she not know how hard he worked to earn the gifts she was so ready to give away? Nadia looked at her parents, icons of wealth and power, and she was ashamed. They were greedy, hollow people with no concern for others. She shouted at them, hurling insults and swearing that when she grew up, she would never be like them. She ran to her room and began throwing her dresses and belongings onto the floor, crying in frustration and anger.

That evening her parents were killed in a car accident

on their way to a dinner engagement. She was sound asleep in her bed and woke to someone calling her name. It was her maternal grandmother. In less than twenty-four hours her life changed forever. The death of her mother and father left Nadia with enough money to never want for anything. Her maternal grandparents moved into the grand estate. Nadia was granted freedoms she had never enjoyed before and was doted on by the elderly couple.

The average Israeli person spends up to two months a year in army reserve duty, and it was expected. When it was Nadia's time to enlist, her grandfather assured her she would not have to serve as he had the means to get the military commitment waived. Nadia rejected his help and joined CHEN, the Women's Corps of the Israel Defense Forces. She worked her way into a combat position, specifically, combat-support, as a weapons trainer.

It was 2011. The Israeli army showed a preference to men at the expense of woman and Nadia was side-lined. She found an assignment with Shabak in the Arab Affairs Department, responsible for Arab-related counter-terrorism activities in Israel, the West Bank, and the Gaza Strip. She was determined that her talents and training would not go waste. As part of the Arab Affairs Department, Nadia was involved in anti-terrorist operations aimed at Arab terrorists. In 2002 Nadia and her partner, a fellow agent, were injured in a suicide attack while waiting for a Palestinian informer. This was early in her career, but the impact still haunted her, she did not trust anyone.

Nadia was fluent in Arabic and was able to pass

herself off as Palestinian and go freely about the West Bank. Part of her recruitment was the ability to infiltrate a Palestinian market and talk to fellow shoppers without raising any suspicions.

In 1984, Nadia had been part of the team responsible for the arrest of two Palestinian hijackers. Once they were incarcerated, she lost interest in the two, moving on to other cases; however, while in prison the two were beaten to death by agents. She later found out that her chief, Avraham Shalom, had ordered the two Palestinians killed and them attempted to cover it up. This revelation did not surprise her, his dedication was deep, but his methods left others questioning his leadership.

In 1995 her team had one job, to protect the Israeli Prime Minister Yitzak Rabin. It was an honor to be trusted to take on such a task, especially for a woman. Unfortunately, a right-wing Israeli extremist made it through all their defenses and killed Rabin. Her boss, Karmi Gillon, resigned as a result of the assassination, and Nadia stepped up as the new lead.

The CIA was known to use enhanced interrogation methods at Guantanamo Bay, and when the news of the torture of prisoners was released, the CIA removed themselves from the spotlight and focused on other areas in the world. What was not commonly known was that they learned the techniques from the Shabak. Human rights groups protested the Shabak and claimed that many prisoners died at their hands or were left paralyzed after a period of detention.

The Shabak denied that these interrogation methods constituted torture and insisted that what was termed

"Moderate or increased physical pressure" were only used when prisoners were thought to have information about imminent terrorist attacks.

Nadia's current mission, and what brought her to the IDEC conference, was the SHABAK Challenge. A group of arch terrorists known as White September; part of the global jihadist movement, believed to be funded by Hezbollah were scheduled to have a meet-up at the conference. Just weeks before they had used the dark-net to declare their intent to inflict a terror attack on Israel similar to the one in 2001 in NYC. They even named the operation "Israeli September 11." Nadia's office received a tip that some of the terrorists had already infiltrated the country.

What Eve did not know was that the Weapons 3D simulation was part of the Israeli technological industry working in conjunction with Shaback to find and wipe out groups like White September. So, like Eve, Nadia would work undercover at IDEC.

When Nadia met Eve, and they bonded in simulated battle, she felt she had met a sister, someone who would risk her life for something they believed in, a fellow warrior wanting to help the less fortunate. She also found those same qualities in John, Eve's father.

Chapter Twenty

Special Agent Joseph Carvallo

Carvallo received a phone call, "We've traced Special Agent Eve Black's phone and she has been in a small town in New Mexico for the last couple days. We can say with the utmost certainty that this is the home of her father, John Michael Black, the man you believe was formally known as Lenard Wilkins." Joe couldn't believe his luck. More than twenty years of his life had been devoted to looking for this man, a Weatherman Underground leader responsible for a series of bombings, jailbreaks, and riots from 1969 through the 1970s.

He took down the address and headed to the airport to catch the first plane to New Mexico. It was nearly six hours later when he got off the plane. He rented a car and found lodging at the Hotel Luna Mystica, a glorified trailer and popular place to stay thanks to the tiny house movement. He had chosen it due to its strategic location. It was situated just a quarter of a mile from the Taos airport, in the middle of nowhere. The next morning, he headed up to Tres Piedras. He knew better than to think the residents of this small village would aid in the capture of Wilkins/Black, so he just wandered around town and ended up at the Chili Line Depot for lunch.

It was there he happened to eavesdrop on a conversation about the Black's place by the tower. He pulled up Google maps on his phone and found the tower. He quickly paid his bill and got up to leave, most of his lunch uneaten, he grabbed a piece of sausage from the plate and ate it as he left the restaurant. It was, barr none, the best he had ever tasted.

He found the only house across from the tower, pulled into the gravel drive and knocked on the door. A young lady answered with two young girls peeking around her. Joe pulled out his badge and said to the pretty brown-haired woman.

"Hello ma'am, I am here to speak with Mr. John Black, is he home?"

"No, sorry, he's not here, you may be able to find him at Kuykendall Lumber down the street."

"Do you mind if I come in and wait for him?"

"I'm sorry sir, I'm not comfortable letting a stranger in, near my girls."

Joe moved as if to step through the door and she slammed it shut. He heard the lock snap into place. "Sir, I said no."

Joe reached inside his jacket and pulled out his service weapon, a Glock Model 22, "Please, let me in ma'am." He was not going give up when he was this close to closing the case, to catching the man that had eluded him throughout most of his career. He did not care if he scared her, or her young girls.

Mari saw the weapon in his hand and decided to open the door. Her daughters started to cry. "Girls, go back in the bedroom and play while I talk to this nice man." She said it loudly.

"I have no plans to hurt you." Joe said through the door. When she opened it, he growled at the girls, "You just stay put. Sit there, all of you, and don't move." He waved the gun at the loveseat by the window. He turned to Mari, "Shut those girls up, their crying will give me a headache." The three sat on the sofa as close to each other as possible. Mari shushed the girls as Joe made his way down the narrow hallway to the bedrooms.

Moments later they heard the muffled sound of a body hitting the floor. Nadia appeared and tossed her keys to Mari, "Take the girls to the community center and find someplace to stay for the night. Don't mention our guest to anyone." Mari had been practicing driving and she believed her skills had improved enough to drive the car down the road on her own. She and the girls grabbed some clothes and took Nadia's car into town. Nadia had already shot off two texts, one to John to come home immediately, and one to Eve, in New York, that they had a problem. Eve responded that she would be there by morning, and John that he would be home in five minutes. When he got there, he found Joe, unconscious on his bedroom floor. "What happened?"

"He's an FBI agent," Nadia showed him the badge, "He drew a gun on Mari and scared the girls, then he came back here so I knocked him out with the lamp."

John couldn't help but notice how calm and matter of fact Nadia seemed. He was glad she was so levelheaded. Obviously, she was capable of quick action in stressful situations, but he decided he needed to know more about her background.

Nadia and John carried the unconscious man down into the bunker and tied him securely. John met Eve at the airport and by the time they arrived at the house they had a plan. In times like this, having a close community paid off.

Eve had called Dr. Marconi on their way to Tres Piedras and stopped at her office to pick up two syringes of Succinylcholine, a short-term paralytic, undetectable in an autopsy. Nadia, Eve, and her father bundled the now conscious, very hostile Carvallo into the passenger seat of his own car. Once there, Eve injected the first syringe and untied him. She massaged his hands to minimize the rope burns, she didn't want them to show up if by any chance an autopsy was performed. Eve then carefully removed the duct tape from his mouth.

"Nadia, follow me in your car." Before Eve started

the car, she retrieved Joe's phone from Nadia and used Joe's fingerprint to unlock it. She glanced through the recent text messages, locating his partner, who Joe had told about the trip to check on John. Eve sent a text, "Mitch, I was wrong, this John Black, is too young to be my guy. I'm heading back to the airport and will brief you on my return." She immediately shut off the phone and tucked it nicely away in Joe's coat pocket.

A few miles away, on highway 64 en route to the airport, Eve recalled a dangerous part of the road that would spell death if someone went around the corner too fast. It would do nicely. When Eve was close to the spot, she pulled out the second syringe and jabbed it into Joe's arm. The drug only had a ten-minute effectiveness and she had to be sure he could not turn the wheel or touch the brakes. He immediately went rigid and it took both Nadia and Eve to get him into the driver seat of the car, seat belt on. They put the car in drive, and with the parking brake engaged, Eve aimed the car toward the deep canyon below Route 64. She pushed Joe's foot onto the gas pedal and released the parking brake. The car lurched off the road, leaving deep tracks in the sand and plummeted down. Seconds later flames leaped from below.

Eve and Nadia headed to the airport, Eve had to fly back to Brooklyn and Nadia had to meet up with the new John Black that would take Eve's fathers identity for the next couple weeks.

While the two women were taking care of Special Agent Carvallo, John was doing his part. The first thing he did was to reach out to his neighbor, Ben Meusser. John wanted Ben to take his place and assume his pseudonym until they could be sure the FBI bought the story that Carvallo's death was an accident/suicide. Ben was too young to be Lenard Wilkins so he would not be in danger of being arrested for Johns past.

Ben's parents were part of the original group that founded the SFH. They were also graduate students with John, but their role in the Weatherman Underground was not as visible as John's, so they were not on the list. It had taken them awhile to call him John. For the longest time they would stumble and call him Lenny. Ben also went to graduate school and was now an assistant professor. Unlike Eve, Ben never felt the need to move away from Tres Piedras and decided to marry and have a family there. He was younger than Eve, one of the children she had helped teach so long ago. She had liked him, he asked a lot of questions, and would often beg her to take him out to the desert with her so he could go fossil hunting.

He met his wife during graduate school and when they first moved back home, the village life was foreign to her, the villagers a bit too odd for her liking. But it had been a few years and she settled in, almost. Children helped. The community as a collective, adored children and a mother in the village ranked much higher than a new wife on the Tres Piedras acceptance scale. Their son and baby girl meant the village would continue.

When Ben agreed to help John, he didn't feel he had a choice, it was what you did. He knew it was an SFH thing and his wife would not understand. He could not say "Honey, our neighbor just killed an FBI agent, so I'm going to go pretend to be him so they don't get caught, and oh, by the way, this requires me to go live, for an unknown length of time, with his beautiful foreign girlfriend." It might be easier to get a divorce.

The only plausible solution was to send her and the children to her parent's home, in Texas. Ben shared his concerns with John, and he agreed that three plane tickets were in order and had them delivered to the Meusser house within the hour. John also purchased plane tickets for Mari and the girls to go to Disney. They would enjoy the vacation and would be away in case something serious went down. Eve shared with the others the protocol the FBI would follow in such an event and gave them an estimated time of arrival for the FBI agents who would be sent to look into the mysterious death of Joe Carvallo.

Now that his temporary replacement was in place, John next had to get on his computer and use his considerable skills to create a flawless new driver license for John Black, with a photo of Ben Meusser.

For a week Ben and Nadia played house. This was necessary because from the moment Ben met Nadia, he was terrified. He had heard rumors about her skill with weapons, in particular knives, and the first few nights in the same house, he woke in a full body sweat, having dreamt that she had snuck into his room and slit his throat.

Nadia's time in Tres Piedras was not a mission sanctioned by her superiors. It was not even something Nadia could discuss with her leadership, but she had not been able to resist the opportunity to get close to a well-known hacker like John, especially while the White September group was still at large. They were known for their technological expertise and her relationship with John might prove invaluable. The pièce de résistance was Eve. An American FBI agent who blurred the lines so readily between legal and illegal, professional and personal, can be easily blackmailed. Nadia's new BFF operated in those gray zones almost constantly.

It did not take long for two FBI agents from the Albuquerque field office to show up and start asking questions. Their first stop was John's place where they met John/Ben Meusser, his lovely girlfriend, Nadia, and Seba. When the agents questioned them about Joe being in town, John/Ben said "Yes, a man fitting his description did show up here. He said he was with the FBI and asked me my name and verification, so I showed him my license. He asked me a few questions about my family and how I met Nadia, and then mentioned he was getting hungry, so I recommended he try out the Chili Line Depot."

Ben gave the two agents a very troubled look, and then lowered his voice, as if hiding what he was about to say from Nadia, and told the two agents, "Between us, something was not quite right with that man. When he took hold of my license, I thought he was having some kind of fit or something. He started shaking, and when he left the house, he slammed the door so hard it nearly came off the hinges. I don't know what he was looking for, nor do I want to know, but I hope he will never be coming back to Tres Piedras."

The two looked knowingly at each other before the taller of the two, presumably the boss, said to John/Ben, "Our colleague was a bit under the weather, he has been on a case nearly all of his life and thought the answer was here. On behalf of the FBI, we apologize for any trouble he may have caused you," he looked over in Nadia's direction, "... and your family."

The agents returned to their car and left. Ben and Nadia watched as they went down the street, and at the corner, turned right. "It looks like they are going to the Chili Depot, I better give them a call." Ben told Nadia.

The two agents did not know Joe Carvallo personally, but they knew of his quest to find Lenard Wilkins. When news of his accident hit HQ, the team was tasked with looking into his death. They had to drive past the accident site and could see how someone unfamiliar with the road could have miscalculated and gone over. The car had burned and did not leave much for an autopsy. After questioning Mr. Black, the agents went to the Chili Line Depot, had lunch, and made inquiries. The information they received was not what they expected.

The manager remembered the man and commented how depressed he looked, "I asked the man, if I could help him with something, but he just looked up at me with sad eyes and said there was nothing I could do."

She then looked up at the two agents and said, "When I heard about his death, I thought maybe it could be a suicide. Was it?"

The taller agent said, "No idea ma'am, we're still investigating."

When the agents questioned other villagers, they heard similar stories. Most everyone had seen him and spoke to him about Black, but he seemed confused because John Black who lived in Tres Piedras was a young man. The agent must have been looking for his father who died several years ago.

Dr. Marconi pulled up records and confirmed that a Jonathan Black had died almost twenty years ago. He had a drinking problem and died of a heart attack. He left behind only one son, John Jr.

As the agents drove back to Albuquerque, they were convinced that Joe must have been so distraught about hitting a dead-end in his decades long search, that he may have driven into the canyon intentionally. Perhaps he just couldn't face his SAC. The agents confirmed with HQ that it was an accidental death. That's all anyone needed to know.

When the drama died down and the special agent's death was down in the books as an accident, normalcy returned to the village of Tres Piedra. Ben Meusser moved back home, and John came out of hiding to find Nadia and Seba anxiously waiting for him. They both showered him with kisses and love. This was not the first time the villagers had banded together to fend off the government. They had been doing it for decades.

Chapter Twenty-One

Wall Street

It had only been a couple months since the conference. Eve was now carrying around two cell phones, one to keep in touch with the conference attendees, registered to Dr. Mathers, and another one that belonged to Eve. Keeping track of which phone and which persona she would be using proved to be a little difficult for Eve. Her brain just didn't work as well as she thought it would when she was "In the moment." Perhaps it was age.

Both Jackson and Campbell texted her with some regularity. If she had to choose between the two, it would definitely be Jackson. Campbell, when compared to Jackson, was still a child. Jackson was also really hot, and skilled in bed, so maybe her opinion was skewed just a little. Eve was happy she lived alone, because there were a couple Skype calls with Jackson that she was pretty sure would not be appreciated by the FBI. Or rather, they may appreciate her willingness to go that far to keep the undercover persona and her contacts.

Jackson kept insisting that they meet up soon, he lived in New York, Nicole recently moved to New York, different Burroughs, sure, but close enough to have a weekend together. Finally, the time was right, and she told Jackson via text that she had a plan. Her publishers needed some more information for the book, and if the four were willing she would like to meet them, and of course compensation would be made at a total of five thousand each, and travel expenses.

Jackson and his posse agreed to the deal and a date was set. On the following Saturday, the four men would stay at the Holiday Inn on Water Street, one block from Wall Street. She would meet them in the lobby and conduct the interview. Nicole and Jackson would have dinner and Nicole told Jackson they could spend that night together, and perhaps another, if time permitted. She asked Jackson to make the room reservations and assured him that upon their arrival she would reimburse him for any and all expenses. Those plans in place, Eve had personal business to attend to.

She chose a Saturday for the big day because most of the Pacific Mutual Insurance employees would have the day off and be away from the office. This wasn't about hurting or killing people; it was about taking out the building, removing it from the Wall Street landscape, and showing other insurance companies that they had to change their ways, or this could happen to them. By eliminating their computer infrastructure, she hoped medical bills, debts, liens, and all insurance records kept by Pacific Mutual would be irretrievable. Eve was convinced that the repercussions of their actions today would more than make up for any lives lost. Her goal was maximum destruction with minimal collateral damage.

Her morning routine differed from the normal workout and breakfast. The week prior, Eve had stopped at a small wig shop and purchased an eight-inch kinky, curly wig specifically designed for ethnic women. She went shopping in a Goodwill and paid the few dollars cash for an appropriate looking out-fit. Once fitted out, Eve was going to channel her best Camilla, accent and attitude, when she arrived at the Holiday Inn hotel, but first she had a stop to make at the Pacific Mutual Insurance Company.

At sixty stories, the PMI building was one of the tallest on Wall Street. The building's footprint was primarily made up of commercial entities; however, there was a chance that there were a few residential apartments on some of the floors. Eve's father had managed to get a blueprint of the building, but no information on occupancies, that being a closely guarded secret. The blueprint helped determine at what location the bomb should be placed to do the most damage. Eve arrived at the main entrance and rapped on the locked door, looking very serious and a little confused.

She could see two security guards inside. She made an exaggerated glance down at her watch-pointed to it, then banged on the door again. She knew if she could see them, they could most definitely see her. Once she managed to get the attention of the two guards, she reached into her pocket and pulled out her FBI badge. She said something they could not hear through the door and pushed her badge against the glass. The two security guards looked at each other. The overweight guy sitting in the chair gave Eve a "What the hell do you want" face, and leaned back in his chair. He leaned a bit too far back and nearly toppled over, but fortunately he caught the edge of the desk and pulled himself up before he made a complete ass of himself in front of the FBI agent. The slender, older guard gave her a smile and rushed over to open the door for her.

"Hello young lady, er...officer, ma'am, what can I do for you today?"

Eve told him that she was scheduled to meet with the CEO, Mr. Jameson, she had Googled him earlier that morning. Eve pretended to be rummaging through her pockets for a business card. "Something about a computer virus attached to an email. I am here to get the full story so I can relay it back to the field office."

The older man ushered her in, but while doing so told Eve that Mr. Jameson was not in, nor was he expected. Damn, she was going to have to do this the hard way, she had so hoped it would have been simpler. She pulled out her Glock and shot the larger man behind the desk, he fell backwards, mirroring his actions just moments before. Eve appreciated that foreshadowing and thought how comical he looked as he fell, like humpty-dumpty. She spun around before the older man understood what was happening and shot him as well. Eve was relieved that the fat one had opted to stay in his seat. She had no problem dragging the thinner guard behind the desk so that neither body would be visible from the street.

Eve carefully placed the backpack, a gift from Vic, next to the interior beam, pointed out by her father as the best location for the blast. How he knew these things, she was not sure. It wasn't likely Eve would ever get around to asking him, she was still an FBI agent after all.

Inside the bag was a bomb, 30kg of plastic explosive with 500 ball bearings, an exact replica of those used by the New York Four. As she headed out the door, she heard moaning from behind the desk. "Bloody hell," she thought. Could she not do anything right? Eve went back and looked at the fat man moaning. Apparently, in her rush to get the job done, she had not aimed correctly and missed his heart. "Rookie mistake," Eve told herself, "When in doubt shoot 'em in the head." She pulled out her gun, aimed carefully this time. A second later, he was dead.

She left Pacific Mutual, making sure she followed the path that kept her away from CCTV, but maintained a casual air. She made her way over to Water Street and to the Holiday Inn. It was only a couple blocks away, but adrenaline was rushing through her bloodstream, her heart rate was up, and her lungs expanded. She was primed and ready to go. Maintaining external calm was nearly impossible, especially for Eve.

The city was crowded, and more than a few people

bumped into her. On any other day knocking into Eve could be hazardous for any pedestrian, but today it was unsafe for her as well. She was carrying another backpack. Inside this one was a second bomb, similar to the first. Eve handed out a few irritated looks but mostly ignored people and made her way to the hotel.

Before going inside Eve shed a layer of clothing, the layer that said FBI, and now she was wearing one that screamed hotel maid. She walked inside. Behaving as if you belong there is the best way to avoid questions when walking into an area that is off limits to the general public. The trick rarely failed, and before she knew it, Eve was in the employee's locker room.

She had two choices, break into a locker and find a uniform, or convince the staff she was one of them and hope they had pity on her and offered up a spare. Eve pretended to rifle through the backpack and managed, with very little trouble, to bring on full crocodile tears. The ladies nearby asked her if she was okay. Eve explained to them that her uniform was at home and without it she could not work, and if she couldn't work, she would not have the money to pay rent, blah blah blah. She was so uninterested in what she was saying that she was not even paying attention to herself.

One of the ladies looked her up and down and said, "You are too fat to wear my uniform, but Juanita can lend you one of hers."

The other woman, presumably Juanita, scowled at the skinny Latina woman and then smiled at Eve, "Sure honey, you can wear one of mine, when does your shift end?"

Eve mentally patted herself on the back for exercising restraint; she did not shoot, stab, or beat up the skinny bitch that just called her fat. She told the kind, plump woman that she was pulling a double and would bring the uniform back clean and pressed in the morning. Eve pulled on the uniform, locked up the backpack and was ready to go do her maid thing.

As she was leaving the locker room, she realized the skinny lady was on the toilet, and the nice one was nowhere to be seen. Eve waited for the stall door to open and she slammed it back on the skinny lady so hard that she flew against the back wall, wailing, "You broke my nose!"

Eve gave her an unapologetic "Lo siento," and proceeded out the door.

She was minding her own business, strolling down the hall with a housekeeping cart that she had snatched from a lower floor, while the maid responsible for the cart was inside a room making the bed. The cart was just to make her look more legitimate as she searched for the New York Four's rooms.

As she proceeded down the hall looking at room numbers a hotel guest walked out of his room, wearing nothing but a towel, and told Eve he needed more towels. Eve gritted her teeth, pasted on a fake smile and in her best Spanish accent (thanks to Camilla) said, "Si senor, un momento, por favor."

He grabbed her arm and said, "NOW!" Clearly this man needed to be taught a lesson, maid persona gone,

FBI training kicked in, and towel man was on the floor, unconscious.

Eve thought to herself "Well hell, what can I do now?" If she left towel man there, her cover would be blown as soon as he woke. Eve searched through the cart until she found a pair of yellow plastic gloves, the kind Camilla would use to wash the dishes and clean the toilets. Eve paused a moment, the dishes and the toilets, why did she never think about how disgusting that was.

Hopefully Camilla owned several pairs and did not mix and match. Eve could not believe how she could get so easily distracted. Dammit, she had work to do. She missed her stepmom intensely and unbidden, real tears started to form. She shook her head and told herself to focus, looking down at the unconscious, but still breathing, hotel guest.

Eve put on the gloves. She dragged towel man into the room and shut the door. Only one side of the bed was disheveled, so he was most likely alone. She heard heavy breathing and very bad acting. Eve looked over at the TV to see a man and several women riding plastic horses on a carousal, in the nude. Yep, the man was watching porn. Most likely he would have tried to get more than a towel from her. Eve headed into the bathroom and turned on the water in the bathtub. Then she dragged the man next to it, removed the towel (without looking, I promise!) and flopped him into the tub. She gave his head a push with her yellow rubber-gloved hands. Before long the gasping ceased, and she had one less thing to worry about.

She glanced over in the mirror and thought to herself, I make a damn fine-looking Latina woman, that skinny maid didn't know what she was talking about.

The last thing Eve did was put out the "do not disturb" sign. She continued down the hallway, pushing the cart and humming to herself Nina Simone's "Take Me to The Water." She thought to herself, "It's going to be a good afternoon, as long as there are no more interruptions."

Eve had received the room numbers from Jackson. They were on the invoice he had texted her for reimbursement. The first room she came to was Bill's. "Such a skinny punk, she recollected, "And ate all the cookies." She liked him the least. It was not just his great metabolism that caused her to dislike him so much, it was his condescending manner, his greater…, okay, fine, it was his metabolism. She knew it was unreasonable, but she smiled to herself, when had anyone accused her of being reasonable?

Bill was the lucky recipient of the gun. The one that Eve had just used to shoot the two security guards. She looked around the room, and finally decided to put it inside the drycleaners bag in the closet. A place she knew he would not notice, but any officer worth their weight in donuts would spot right away. Eve fantasized about leaving Bill a box of poisoned donuts, but with her luck the police officers would help themselves and she would have even more deaths on her hands.

 In Jim's room, she left the backpack with the second bomb. It wasn't that she didn't like him, in fact she did harbored little guilt because she would be the reason these men were finally behind bars. Eve thought back on the CCTV footage of the four planting the bombs in the two cars in front of the synagogue, and the lack of remorse they showed in the court room. They were so busy proving entrapment that people forgot that they actually planted the bombs. The FBI informant may have paved the way for them to do so, but they had no problem killing a few Jews in exchange for a quarter of a million dollars.

When she walked into Jackson's room, she thought about the night they had spent together. Eve would not be opposed to another sleepover with him. He was a very sexy man, and she had enjoyed their time together. She put his Oakleys on the dresser. She skipped Payton's room. He had cleaned up his life and she had respect for his choices. Unlike the other three, he seemed to know how lucky he was and refused to waste his life.

All that work left her feeling a little decaffeinated. The Starbucks nearby was not one of her favorites, but it did give her a nice view of Wall Street, and she knew their coffee would be good. She ordered her usual, a Grande Sumatra, and this time she actually smiled at the young person taking her order. Nothing could spoil her mood today. Eve looked around the room and found the perfect seat near the wall in the back. There was always a chance that the blast could reach this part of Wall Street and blow out the windows. She felt relatively safe between the wall and the bathroom. When she got the text from Jackson saying the four were at the hotel, the next part of her plan began.

She first called her father, but hung up the phone before he answered, as had been prearranged. She knew he wouldn't answer, because the call was the signal to release a computer virus that he had been working on since Camilla's death. Her father had designed a virus constructor, a malicious program that can create new viruses with an interface that allows it to choose the characteristics of the created malware. Inside the constructor was a signature file that spread along with any created viruses.

He sent the constructor into the dark web, knowing that within hours his fellow hackers would be spreading viruses all over the internet. In addition to the virus constructor, he designed a virus with the same signature files that would target the PMI Company's cloud servers and storage. It would take the FBI several years before they could isolate the information needed to identify the maker. John had tried to explain the mechanism behind the virus and constructor, but she did not have the patience to listen nor the know-how to understand. It really didn't matter, as long as he knew what he was doing, and there was nothing to lead the investigation back to him or to her.

She then dialed a second number. This call would also not be answered because it was ringing to a cell phone inside the bomb, still lying on the floor next to the two dead security guards. It rang, rang some more, then an unusual buzzing started to come out of the phone. WTF? She looked down at the number. Damn, she had misdialed. It was a fax line. Seriously, do people still use faxes? Eve called the number again, this time punching each number carefully as she said them in her head.

In a matter of seconds, she heard the explosion. It was so loud that the building shook, and for a moment Eve thought it was going to collapse. The windows cracked, and everyone moved close to the walls, next to her, crowding her. Eve couldn't breathe. The people were too close, she had to get outside, but she knew it was too soon. She rushed to the bathroom, but the door was closed and there were others outside waiting to get in. She pulled out her badge, pushed them aside and banged on the door.

A young man was still pulling up his pants as he walked out of the bathroom looking frightened. She shoved him out of her way, went in, and locked the door. She pulled up the news on her cell phone, and checked social media to see if her father had been successful in planting rumors that the New York Four were responsible for the Wall Street explosion. She leaned against the sink and waited.

Eve left the bathroom when she could no longer hear the voices of panicked Starbucks customers outside the door. Her sense of accomplishment was almost euphoric. Months of planning culminated in this, the destruction of the Pacific Mutual Insurance Company.

Eve and her father had planned this the evening they returned home from the hospital; the night Camilla died. This was their tribute to the woman who took such good care of them, who showed them both love and affection, even when they were unable to reciprocate. They wanted to annihilate Pacific Mutual Insurance and warn other insurance companies that their time was limited. As she walked toward the door of the coffee shop, no one even looked in her direction. She was invisible, just how she liked it.

When Eve stepped out onto the sidewalk, alarms were blaring, and people were running and shouting. A cloud of dust and smoke hung in the air over the rubble of the destroyed building and reduced visibility to a few feet. Invisible fumes made the air acrid and hot in her mouth. Eve was seized coughing. Another rookie mistake, staying so close to the scene of the crime? Maybe, but she smiled through her discomfort.

She may not be the best FBI agent in town, but she sure as hell pulled this one-off right under their noses. She covered her mouth and nose with her sleeve and hurried down the sidewalk. A helicopter was somewhere overhead and as she passed the shops, she saw screens inside with images of the ruined building. She paused briefly at a storefront with several TVs in the display window all tuned to different stations. The reporters were all saying the same thing; The New York Four had struck Wall street. She slowed her pace as she got further away, and the air cleared. She hummed to herself Bob Dylan's song, "Subterranean Homesick Blues."

OPERATION DEEP DIVE:
A STEP INTO THE PAST

Chapter One

So It Begins

Eve was confronted by the intense sunlight the minute she opened the door and walked outside. Her eyes closed to a squint, and she was blinded, causing her to stumble, with a nearby column stopping her fall. She paused, waiting for her eyes to recover, walking to the mailbox should not be dangerous. The hike was short so she had not bothered to grab her sunglasses, a staple for every good FBI agent. It was a beautiful sunny day, but it's Alabama, almost every day is a beautiful, sunny, humdrum, boring kind of bloody day. They lived on a quiet cul-de-sac, in the heart of Cottage Hill, near Mobile. On the upside, the stroll to the mailbox was her chance to breathe without the children at her side.

She looked about with satisfaction at the man-made order she witnessed, seven nearly identical cookie cutter homes with manicured lawns, clean sidewalks, dedicated flower gardens, landscaping, with every home complimenting the other. The community was new but designed to look like old money plantation homes.

You did not find this kind of living in New York City. Real estate costs were so much less in Alabama, Eve was able to buy a home for the same monthly cost of her rental in Brooklyn. Not that money was a real issue for them, Franklin's mother came from a wealthy family and she was forever showering them with gifts of money, vehicles, anything they could ask for. Even with the cleanliness and order all around her, she could not recall a time in her life in which she felt so underwhelmed.

Eve walked with great care, missing the cracks, god knows why, probably haunts from childhood when she was afraid if she stepped on one, she would hurt her mother's back, thus not giving her mother the opportunity to return to Eve and her father. You don't have a lot of sidewalks in the deserts, yet her mother never returned to them. Stupid superstitions, yes, but she continued to step carefully until she reached the mailbox.

It never failed. Eve's eagerness as she readied herself to open the black box, a door to the unknown. It was subtle, the extra pep in her step, an alertness with just a twinge of excitement, she was about to have contact with the outside world. With someone other than her husband, the nanny, her newborn, and the mini-Eve toddler running about inside.

As expected, there were several pieces of mail, different colors, sizes, and weights. A quick run through indicated that at least half of them were junk, the other half, bills. All of it required a more thorough investigation. Eve was in the last month of her three-month maternity leave and she was stir crazy.

She made it back in the two-story colonial and slipped off her shoes just in time to hear her two-year-old daughter, Harper, tiptoeing down the open-tread staircase. Supported only by the spindles, because at only three-foot-tall, she was too short to reach the handrail. She mastered going up the stairs this way much sooner than moving down them. Harper was sporting her favorite superman pajamas, pretending to fly. Eve could not help but smile, she remembered those days, when she had an imagination and believed being a superhero was possible.

Her husband, Franklin, was the decorator in the family and the home reflected it. All that talk about not enjoying growing up in England in his parent's drafty estate home during their first date was clearly a lie because everything in the home screamed British colonialism. Teak woods, textiles printed with exotic patterns depicting local scenes, flora and fauna, and the beautifully aged and well-traveled gorgeous chocolate and tan leather trunks with brass buckles and clasps. Eve didn't mind; she liked the style; It evoked a bygone era that was genteel and elegant while at the same time appearing relaxed and comfortable.

The nursery followed through with the same theme.

In place of the mahogany and brown finishes found in the rest of the home, in this room, dedicated to children and play, they had fresh whites and soft grays, to include: stained white hardwood floors, ceiling fans, and, in place of curtains or blinds, they mounted plantation shutters. The room boasted a rattan rocking chair, a simple canopy bed with make shift rails for Harper, and a white teak crib for Franklin.

The floors were littered with plush rugs, colorful print oversized pillows, and stuffed exotic animals of all sizes. A crayon-decorated white bookcase was home to books, puzzles, and board games. Trunks contained each one of the toys that could fit. The other larger ones, like her doll house and baby doll kitchen, were kept well-ordered and off the floor, and Eve accepted no excuses for it to be otherwise. Harper was transitioning into a big kid bed, so she had access to her play things throughout the night, and on more than one occasion Eve woke to Harper in the nursery singing and playing by herself in the early morning hours.

They hired a maid that showed up after breakfast and tidied up the place. She left before Eve returned from the gym, making life more tolerable. Eve had no idea kids could be so messy. Back at the SFH commune, there were very few young people and cleanliness seemed to be a priority for all the residents. Sure, there were one or two people that were just a little "unique" in their attire and space, but they were oddities, not the norm.

Eve opened the refrigerator and pulled out a jug of unsweetened organic apple juice and filled a sippy cup for Harper. She had to give it a taste, it sounded awful, and she wondered what kind of person drank unsweetened juice? Her first thought was to spit it out into the sink, but she managed to swallow. That was unpleasant. Eve couldn't believe her daughter drank that stuff.

After distracting Harper with a video and snacks she sat down at the table, ready to sort through the mail. The amount of paper waste annoyed Eve, do people not understand it's the electronic age? The stack was high, so she categorized the piles into junk, bills, and other. She found one of particular interest. It was a 5 x 7 Manila envelope, with a disk and string closure, and no return address. How fascinating.

Eve opened it carefully. She did this because she had a fear of paper cuts, not out of worry that she might damage the contents. Paper cuts were the absolute worst. Eve was certain that she would rather take a bullet than have a paper cut. But, she supposed, it depended on where the shot entered her body. Ugh, Eve admonished herself because of how easily she could be sidetracked. She stared back down at the contents of the envelope.

What she pulled out of that envelope was a series of photos of herself from three years ago. Eve, as a rule, tried, albeit unsuccessfully, to hide her emotions. But alone in the kitchen, looking at the photos that would likely change her life, left her exposed. The tingling started at her toes and spread throughout her body. A smile cracked her face and she was feeling bubbly, her mind was racing, her heartbeat was thumping so loud she was sure everyone in the house could hear it. She just had a good feeling about the day. Eve dropped the packet, and the pictures back onto the table, got up abruptly, and made herself a cup of coffee. She then stood at the counter looking at the items and then sat back down.

She picked up the photos, one at a time. The images were clear, very professional, not a product of CCTV. In one photo she could make out her own face, under the curly wig, on the street outside the hotel. In another, she was holding the gun used to shoot the security officers. A third photo was a picture of Eve with a backpack containing the bomb that would cause the destruction of the insurance company on Wall Street. There were more, all of them showing Eve on that eventful day.

None of this was sanctioned by the FBI, because as we all know, the FBI does not sanction killing, that's exclusive to the CIA. This was part of a plot by Eve and her dad as an homage to her stepmother, and a warning to other insurance agencies, *change your ways or you will be next*. In other words, yes, based on the definition of terrorism, Eve was a domestic terrorist, but this was a one time thing, not a career.

---To Be Continued--

CPSIA information can be obtained
at www.ICGtesting.com
Printed in the USA
JSHW010009290520
5940JS00006BA/44